# A chill ran up

Thinking how cl... victim nearly un... was safe in town... Julia had come the closest of everyone he knew to being at the wrong end of the arsonist's match. A fierce need to protect her, to be sure she was far from danger, rose in his chest.

"Come up to the cabin in the morning," he said, trying to keep the urgency, the worry, from his voice. "A day out in the woods with me and Ginny might be just the stress reliever you need."

She worried her bottom lip. "Okay, but only for one day."

Thank God she'd said yes. At least for one day he'd know where she was, and he wouldn't worry. All three of them—Mike, his daughter and Julia—would be far from town, nestled deep in Mount Pine.

"Want me to help you close up? Walk you to your car?"

She hesitated, then glanced out the window at the charred skeleton of the building next door. "I would like that. Even in broad daylight it's hard to feel..."

"Safe," Mike finished. He couldn't agree more.

**Shirley Jump** is an award-winning, *New York Times*, *Wall Street Journal*, Amazon and *USA TODAY* bestselling author who has published more than eighty books in twenty-four countries. Her books have received multiple awards and kudos from authors such as Jayne Ann Krentz, who called her books "real romance," and Jill Shalvis, who called her book "a fun, heartwarming small-town romance that you'll fall in love with." Visit her website at shirleyjump.com for author news and a booklist, and follow her on Facebook at Facebook.com/shirleyjump.author for giveaways and deep discussions about important things like chocolate and shoes.

### Books by Shirley Jump

### Love Inspired Cold Case

*After She Vanished*

Visit the Author Profile page
at LoveInspired.com for more titles.

# Refuge
# Up in Flames

*New York Times* Bestselling Author

## SHIRLEY JUMP

LOVE INSPIRED
INSPIRATIONAL ROMANCE

## LOVE INSPIRED®

### INSPIRATIONAL ROMANCE

Recycling programs
for this product may
not exist in your area.

ISBN-13: 978-1-335-42620-8

Refuge Up in Flames

Love Inspired
22 Adelaide St. West, 41st Floor
Toronto, Ontario M5H 4E3, Canada
www.LoveInspired.com

**Printed in U.S.A.**

Beloved, let us love one another:
for love is of God; and every one that loveth
is born of God, and knoweth God.
—*1 John 4:7*

To my husband,
the hero I always dreamed of
and never believed existed until now.
I am blessed to have you in my life.

# Chapter One

Some mornings, the wind whistled sharply through Crooked Valley, an angry sprite charging its way up the Rocky Mountains. Other mornings, the air was as still as a bobcat on the hunt, holding a hint of anticipation in the striated clouds. On all mornings, warm, cold, sunny, windy or rainy, Mike Byrne spent a little time on the deck of his little house nestled into the hill at the end of a cul-de-sac. Today, a winter storm was beginning to gather strength, and all that turbulence made Mike wish he could do his life over, somehow change the course of events that had left him a widowed single father who was better at relating to German shepherds than his own daughter.

Dogs, cats, even birds, had very few expectations and rarely asked more from him than he could give. It was why he had become a veterinarian, shifting his plans in college from people medicine to animal medicine, when he'd realized his bedside manner wasn't exactly warm and fuzzy. For most of his career, that had served him well. Animals loved him, and people put up with his gruff exterior because they knew their Maltese or Siamese was in good hands. Veterinary school had prepared him for a whole host of emergencies, from breeched puppies to broken wings, but it hadn't taught him a thing about how to go on after his wife's car was T-boned and then skidded off an icy road, crashing into a concrete wall.

That had been a year and a half ago, and a better man might have figured out how to be both mother and father to Ginny. But there weren't any college classes he could take or certifications he could pursue that would fill the yawning chasm left by Mary's death. Praying seemed pointless, because he couldn't understand how God could take the one beautiful thing in Mike's life and the most important thing in Ginny's life. And so Mike fumbled along, only finding his footing in the hours when he was at work.

The practice was growing at a fast clip, as more and more people settled in sleepy Crooked Valley. With the growth in work-at-home jobs, thousands of people had left Denver and other big cities in their rearview mirrors, seeking the idyllic small-town life. Mike had lived in Crooked Valley for ten years, coming here with his new wife to take over a practice from a retiring veterinarian, and had always thought the town had the perfect mix of charm and community.

Until the last few months. Now, Crooked Valley had become a place no one recognized anymore.

Outside his veterinary office, he heard the growing cry of the fire department's sirens, the sound so familiar it seemed like a creepy soundtrack for the town. Two trucks, an engine and an ambulance rushed by his downtown office in a whir of lights and noise. The much-too-frequent sound chased a shiver down Mike's spine.

"I sure hope it's not another one," said Jamie, who was promoted to Mike's veterinary assistant a year ago. He was a young kid who had started out as an intern and never left. Jamie was enthusiastic and gentle, and a sucker for Labradors.

*Another one* meant another arson. Crooked Valley had had five of them in the last six months. The first had been an abandoned warehouse, then an office building closed for the weekend then an auto garage that had just opened the week before. The two after that had been homes where the residents had thankfully gotten out in time. But as the arsonist got closer and closer to actually hurting someone, everyone in Crooked Valley tensed when they heard the sirens.

For months, the tiny Crooked Valley Fire Department had tried to put the pieces together themselves. The first couple of buildings had been attributed to teenage kids getting into trouble. The garage was initially thought to have been started by an overturned gas can, but when the two houses were hit, the CVFD had revisited the investigations of all the fires that had happened in the previous months. They'd waited a long time to call in help from the state arson investigator, which wasn't a surprise to Mike, even if he disagreed with the decision. In Crooked Valley, people took care of their own, an attitude that extended to law enforcement as much as it did to residents.

"Those sirens could mean anything." Mike and Jamie crossed to the front windows. Mike prayed Jamie was wrong, that this fire wasn't purposely set. "A grease fire in a kitchen or—" The fire chief's truck passed by, then a white car marked Arson Investigator, followed by two police cars.

"Or another one," Jamie finished.

"Whoever is doing this, let's pray they catch him soon," Mike said. He reached for the door of Room Three. "Oh, and can you check on Mrs. Larson's cat? He should be coming around from surgery about now."

Back to work and back to the part of his mind that was able to compartmentalize everything else, stuffing all his emotions and worries into a mental closet. Mike stepped into the exam room, and greeted Henry Rathburn and his mom, Sarah. "How are you?"

"Good, Doc. But Scotty is having trouble again," Sarah said, gesturing toward the squat tan-and-white corgi sprawled on the cool stainless-steel table. Sarah and Henry had been in Mike's office several times, between Scotty the corgi and Midnight, their cat, who had a penchant for eating paper and yarn. Scotty was twelve years old, a good dog with a loyal heart, whose back legs were now nearly immobile. He'd gone from a bounding puppy to a meandering geriatric to a pained elderly dog who had no get up left in his go.

"Let's check you out," Mike said to the dog. Scotty barely reacted as Mike checked his heart rate, drew some blood and palpated his stomach. Just two months ago, the corgi had been happier and more active. "You're doing great, buddy," he said to the dog. "Just great." The dog's tail gave a couple solid thumps.

For ten years, Mike had served as the lone vet in Crooked Valley, following in his grandfather's steps. Mike had grown up around animals, helping out at his grandfather's practice in St. Louis for years, before heading off to get his degree. By that time, his grandfather had sold his practice. When Mike got married, Mary wanted to live closer to her family in Denver, so they'd settled in Colorado, lucking into a practice that was available, which gave Mike a head start on setting up his own vet office. It hadn't taken long for Mike to be completely charmed by the weather, the people and the lifestyle here.

The practice had done well over that decade. Nearly every animal in this town nestled at the foot of the Rockies came to his office, which meant he knew pretty much everyone who lived in a thirty-mile radius. Including the very worried little boy and his mom who sat on the wooden bench against the wall, watching and waiting for good news that Mike wasn't sure he had. He bit back a sigh.

Mike came around the table to bend down in front of the boy.

"Is he okay?" Henry asked, the words quavering on the end of his lips.

"Scotty is quite old now, Henry, and being a senior citizen comes with a number of issues," Mike said.

The towheaded boy, just a little younger than Ginny, nodded. "He's older than me. And I'm five." He held up a grubby, chubby hand and splayed his fingers.

"When a dog gets older, especially a corgi, they can develop something called degenerative myelopathy. It's a disease that affects their spinal cord and often leads to paralysis."

Henry gave Mike a blank look. Every time he had to talk to a patient's owner, Mike struggled to explain big concepts like life and death and progressive diseases. Heck, he struggled to talk to people in general.

Outside the windows of the exam room, the snow that had been a few flakes began to fall faster and thicker.

Sarah turned and took Henry's hand in her own. "You know how Grandpa has trouble sometimes making his birdhouses and he has you hold the tools? That's kind of the same thing that Scotty has. His legs have trouble working, just like Grandpa's hands."

Henry swiveled back to Mike. His big brown eyes welled and his lower lip trembled. "Can you fix him?"

Mike's heart squeezed. He knew what it was like to lose a pet, or worse, to watch one slowly decline until you had to make difficult choices. He'd had to put down his own beloved dog two years ago, and it had been one of the hardest decisions of his life.

Mike wanted to tell Henry that losing a pet was bad, but it wasn't the worst thing that could happen to a person. Mike knew worse, and he wouldn't wish that on his most hated enemy.

Right now, though, Scotty was Henry's whole world. The corgi followed Henry around from dawn to dusk, slept in Henry's bed and sat at his feet during dinner. He was more friend than pet, and the family wasn't ready to say goodbye. Which meant Mike needed a solution.

"Scotty's really struggling," Mike said to Henry, and flicked a glance at Sarah. What the corgi had was only going to get worse, leading to total paralysis. He could tell neither Scotty nor Henry was ready for Scotty's life to be over. Besides, Mike had seen enough death in the last two years. He wasn't going to let this dog go, too. As a teenager, Mike's golden retriever had been his best friend, and sometimes the only thing that got him through the hard days. When Bandit died, Mike had struggled with the thought of another pet. Six months later, Mary had died, and adding a pet to days that were filled with grief and difficult choices seemed like a bad decision. So for now, the Byrne house was a pet-less house.

Scotty was clearly Henry's best buddy and, from what Sarah had told Mike when she saw him in the grocery store last week, a huge comfort during these scary days when it seemed like the whole town was on fire. Arson wasn't something any child should have to think about, which meant helping him get his best buddy back to moving. "I'm going to do whatever I can to help Scotty. I think I have a way to make him regain some mobility."

A little light appeared in Henry's eyes. "And he can run with me in the park again?"

"Maybe." It depended on the dog as much as it did the device. Mike straightened, then went back to the dog. Scotty had his head on his paws, his dark brown eyes fixed on the blank green walls. The dog didn't understand why his legs had stopped working and why he couldn't do the things he used to do with the boy he loved most in the world. Mike gave the corgi a rub behind the ears.

"I'm going to have someone I know see if he can build a feasible ambulatory solution for Scotty," Mike explained. He retrieved a tape measure from the drawer and measured the width between Scotty's hips, the length of his front legs and his back legs and the length of his spine, then jotted all the information on a spare prescription pad.

After coming home from the war, Mike's neighbor Calvin Moretti had talked about setting up a side business building custom gadgets but had yet to make any moves to start. Cal had been depressed, understandable given the tough time he'd had after his Humvee struck an IED. Maybe this small project would be enough to help the wounded vet give back after he returned from Bethesda by way of Afghanistan. He'd been unable to run his machine shop full-time, and to Mike, that left Cal with too much time to think and grieve. This project would be as good for Cal as it would be for Scotty, and given what

Mike had seen thus far of Cal's talents, he had no doubt his friend could create something workable. "I can't guarantee anything, but my opinion is that a device like this can assist Scotty's movement. His front legs have yet to be affected by this degenerative disease. I'm hopeful we can replicate the movement of his rear legs."

Henry kept blinking.

"What kind of device are you talking about, Doc?" Sarah asked.

Once again, Mike had relied on the crutch of medical jargon. His late wife had teased him about being a man of few words—few regular words—but many, many complicated words. In the dark of night, when he questioned a universe that would take sweet Mary and leave him fumbling through life, he wondered if she had been happy. His loving wife, who had believed until the day she died that his heart was there. *One of these days, Tin Man,* she used to say, *you'll open up that heart of yours. I plan on being here when you do.*

Except she wasn't here. And he hadn't had the chance to open his heart and tell her how much he loved her before she died. She'd left the house that morning with a kiss and her soft *I love you,* and all he'd been able to say was goodbye, already distracted by the charts he'd brought home to work on after hours. They'd argued often about his difficulty opening up, and every time, Mike had promised to be better, to try harder. It wasn't that he didn't feel love for his wife; it simply wasn't his instinct to speak the words. The hurt on her face, a hurt he had seen a hundred times before, haunted him every night.

Why couldn't he say those three words she had longed to hear? Why did he retreat, again and again, behind clinical language and impersonal topics instead of speaking the truth?

Mike cleared his throat. Chased the thoughts to the back of his mind and shut them behind a firm mental door. "Sorry for getting so technical. I mean a device with wheels that can do the work of Scotty's legs."

"Like a wheelchair?" Henry looked confused. "Do I gotta push him around?"

"Not exactly. The dog's movements will be under his own power. And dependent upon his motivation." Mike ran a hand down the dog's head and back. Scotty let out a sigh, but otherwise didn't move. Poor thing was so depressed, and with good reason. Mike would have to see if Cal could turn this around fast. "Give me a few days, and when you bring Scotty back, hopefully we'll have an option for him."

"I'm gonna pray real hard for Scotty." Henry popped to his feet, his entire face changed by this potentially good news. That smile, coupled with the happy wag of Scotty's tail, *that* was why Mike kept showing up to work, kept on trying until he'd tried every possible option. "And then I'm gonna take real good care of him. And I'm gonna get him a cheeseburger. Scotty likes cheeseburgers."

Mike gave the chubby, much-loved corgi a glance. "Scotty should be eating dog food, Henry. People food is for people."

"Okay." Henry peered into the dog's face. For the first time since he'd arrived, Scotty perked up. His tail thumped twice, and he leaned into the boy's touch. "You're gonna get wheels, Scotty, and then we're gonna go to the park and go to the liberry and play in the yard."

Henry's mother laughed. "One thing at a time, Henry. Let's get Scotty home first. Okay?" She scooped up the dog and cradled him to her chest. "Thanks, Doc. You have no idea what this means to Henry."

"Scotty's part of the family. And no one wants to lose part of their family." Mike took a breath and shook his head. He hadn't meant to let that slip. "The four-legged members, I'm talking about right now. Not the…" His voice trailed off, and the rest of the words in his mouth got jumbled together.

"Of course." Henry's mother nodded and averted her gaze. Like most people in Crooked Valley, there was that uncomfortable moment when the death of Mary came up, and people didn't know what to say. *Sorry* seemed so useless, especially a year and a half later, when Mike was still struggling.

"I will relay an ETA on the device when I have one," Mike said, to change the subject before she offered to bake him a pie or a tuna casserole. His freezer was filled to the brim with good intentions. "And I'll make sure his heartworm preventative prescription is ready when you check out."

The trio headed to the front, and Mike dipped into the back hall. He could hear the storm picking up, the wind nipping at the building, and he hoped the strong wind wasn't exacerbating the fire. There were days when Mike was afraid Crooked Valley was one good breeze away from a town-wide fire.

Mike opened the medicine chest and was reaching for the tiny flea, tick and heartworm chewable tablets when his office manager came up beside him. She wore that look on her face that Mike knew too well. "Again?"

Keesha nodded. Smart, enthusiastic and given to wearing cartoony zoo-animal-printed scrubs—which the clients always loved—Keesha had been with Mike for three years after vet tech school and three years as a volunteer before that. Her black hair was straightened and in a tight ponytail today, and she wore only the minimum of makeup on her face. "Sorry. I rescheduled the next two appointments to give you time to get over there."

*Again.*

Mike sighed. These phone calls were becoming a far-too-regular occurrence. Mike finished filling a bag, then handed it to Keesha. "This is for Scotty Rathburn out front. Tell them I will reach out when I have a date for them to come back in."

"Will do, Dr. Byrne. Do you want me to cancel the rest of your day?"

"No. I'll figure out something." As he had for the last year and a half, sort of pasting a life together out of glue and hope and a lot of mistakes. Mike tugged on his jacket, a thick brown Carhartt that kept the worst of the Colorado winter off his back, then headed out to his Jeep.

The ride to Crooked Valley Elementary only took a few minutes. The clouds hovering above the mountains loomed dark and thick, already dumping the predicted three to six inches before dinnertime. Followed by another cold front and potential storm at the end of the week, with one warm day peppered in the middle. Welcome to the unpredictable weather of Colorado. Sunny almost every day, and a roller coaster of temperatures from one day to the next.

He wouldn't want to live anywhere else. Colorado was the place that held Mike's best memories—and his worst ones. Maybe a less masochistic man would move, but he wanted Ginny to look back someday and see the mountains and the trails and the rivers and see her mother in them.

He walked into the school and didn't even have to announce himself at the door. The secretary, Francine Wilcox, buzzed him in and gave him a weak smile. "She's in with Principal Conley."

Mike nodded. "Thanks, Francine. How's your goldendoodle?"

"Spunky as ever. Smart as a whip, too. Thanks for the recommendation of that trainer. It's made a world of difference."

Mike just nodded. He wasn't good at the small-talk thing. Didn't waste time on commenting about the weather or the price of coffee at the grocery store. In a crowd, he went positively mute. He hated the entire process of meeting new people, pretending to care about where they went to college or what part broke on their car, then returning the volley with some clever attempt at conversation. His mother had called him shy; his father had said he was an *embarrassing disgrace*. Mike figured he was somewhere in the middle, more like *painfully introverted but trying to pretend he wasn't*.

Mike ducked past the half wall that divided the front office, then stopped to knock on Don Conley's door. Even though they were both in their thirties now, it was weird to see *Principal* next to Don's name. They'd met when Mike first moved here and had joined the men's baseball league. The two of them had played together every spring—Mike as third baseman, Don as pitcher—and had shared more memories than either of them could recount. Their wives had been friends, and before Mary died, the four of them had spent many a Sunday afternoon together.

"Come in," Don called out.

Mike entered, and saw Ginny sitting in a wooden chair much too big for her, swinging her legs back and forth. She had a bandage on her knee that hadn't been there this morning and a scrape on her left elbow. The bright pink cast on her right arm had a smudge above her thumb and another on the end. There was dirt in her hair—which wasn't as much of a tangled mess today thanks to a cookie bribe this morning—and the hem of her pink dress was torn. Her Hello Kitty backpack sat in her lap, undoubtedly stuffed with whatever she needed to go home, three hours after she arrived at school. Mike bit back a sigh and dropped into the other chair. "How you doing, Ginny?"

"Fine." She kept her gaze on her feet as they swung forward, then disappeared under the chair. Back and forth, back and forth.

"We seem to be having some…anger management problems," Don said.

"Another fight at recess?"

Don nodded. "Mrs. Henneman said Ginny needs to learn to control her temper or she'll not be welcome back to class. And I hate to say it, Mike, but I agree with the teacher in this case."

Mrs. Henneman was close to seventy, maybe even eighty—no one knew because she never told anyone her age—and had been teaching at Crooked Valley Elementary for decades. He'd heard that she was a tough taskmaster who didn't allow the kids in her classroom to get out of hand. He wasn't surprised she'd said that about Ginny, because if there was one phrase that would describe his daughter, it was *out of hand.*

"Becky started it," Ginny grumbled. "She said I looked dumb with my cast, and she made fun of me because I couldn't throw the ball."

Mike met Don's gaze over the desk. Don gave him a sad nod. "We're going to talk about this when we get home, Ginny."

"Fine." She clutched her backpack tighter to her chest. Avoiding looking at him, just as she had for the past year and a half. Even when she fell off the swings and broke her wrist last month, she'd been stoic and distant in the emergency room. "Can I go now?" A pause, then a begrudgingly uttered "Please?"

Don nodded. "Ginny, why don't you wait in the office with Mrs. Wilcox? I'm going to talk to your dad for a second."

As soon as the door shut behind Ginny, Mike leaned forward, propping his elbows on his knees. "I'm sorry, Don. Ever since her mother died, Ginny has been angry at the world. At me. At anyone and everything." It was the excuse Mike had been using with everyone, and especially with Don. Maybe he should look into a new therapist or something for Ginny. She was clearly having trouble moving on and processing.

To be honest, they both were.

"I get it. I do." Don gave him that same look of sympathy that Sarah Rathburn had delivered a few minutes earlier. The helpless, what-do-I-say face that Mike had seen a hundred times in the receiving line at the funeral home. As if Mike was going to supply just the right platitude? How could he? He'd barely survived those three days between the accident and the burial, never mind the eighteen months after that.

"But," Don went on, "you understand why we can't have that disruption in the classroom? She argues with Mrs. Henneman over everything from sitting at her desk to what color pencil she's supposed to use to shade a tree."

"I'm sorry, Don." Mike had started saying *sorry*

all the time, too, by way of explaining, *I know my kid is out of hand, but I don't know how to fix it.*

Don picked up a small white card on his desk. "I know Ginny is dealing with the broken wrist, too, which adds more to a plate that's already full. You might want to give Julia Beaumont a call. She's an occupational therapist who works with kids. My sister used her last year when my nephew broke his leg and had to miss the entire soccer season. She said Julia totally turned my nephew's attitude around."

Mike took the card. Simple, clean font. Just her name, title and number. "Beaumont. Isn't that the family who owns that coffee shop downtown?"

"Yeah. Julia works there part-time. But mostly she does this OT thing with kids. It might be worth a shot."

"I've tried everything, you know. Counseling, that grief camp last summer, talking to her… It's like she's gone someplace I can't get her back from."

Don sighed, and the lines of sympathy deepened. "If there's one thing I've learned as a principal, Mike, it's that you can always get them back, especially if you ask God for help. Sometimes you just gotta reach deeper."

Maybe. That probably only worked if there was a relationship buried somewhere under all of that. Mike loved his daughter, but Mary had been the one who had been close to Ginny. The one Ginny reached for, over and over again, to hold, soothe, love. Mike had no clue how to do that. With Mary's parents out of town for the winter, he had also lost the crutch of

Grandma and Grandpa. It was all on Mike's shoulders. "Thanks, Don. Again."

"Anytime." Don rose and came around his desk. "How about you? You doing okay?"

"Me? I'm fine. Just fine." It was the lie he'd been telling himself and all those *I'm sorry* people for a year and a half. Maybe if he told it often enough, he'd start to believe it himself.

# Chapter Two

Julia Beaumont wound her way down the long, slop-ing road that led from her apartment to downtown Crooked Valley. The snow that had started an hour ago was starting to thicken, and she whispered a quick prayer for safe roads. It was mid-December, and the air was brisk with the first kiss of winter. The snowy caps of the Rockies watched over the town and the sparkling lake that lay to the west. A breathtaking view that passed by Julia's windows unnoticed. Stress curled a tight fist into her stomach.

In the last few months, Julia's occupational ther-apy business had taken a nosedive, on purpose. She'd stopped accepting new clients, canceled appoint-ments and dropped as far off the radar as she could. After what happened—

Was she even in the right profession anymore? Did she have any business helping other people? Maybe God didn't mean for her to do something else. *But what, God? What am I meant to be?*

There were no answers in the falling snow. Ahead, the turnoff from Red Rock Road and onto Golden Byway loomed. Julia's throat closed, her stomach clenched and a fine sweat broke out on her brow. For six months, Julia had avoided that turn, instead looping down to Canyon Way, a two-mile detour to downtown. She was already running late for her shift at the coffee shop, and that would make Chloe late for her doctor's appointment. Her little sister was counting on Julia to be responsible and be where she promised she would be, and Julia didn't want to let her down again. Julia should just take the turn and get over it.

She slowed at the light, merging into the right-hand lane. *It'll be all right. It's just a street, nothing more.* Red shifted to green, and Julia hesitated. There was a sharp honk from the pickup truck behind her, and she jerked forward, making the turn, halfway through it before she realized she couldn't do it. Couldn't pass this house again.

There were cars behind her, which meant she had nowhere to go but forward. The driver of the red pickup laid on his horn, an irate, annoying sound. Julia gripped the steering wheel so hard the leather-covered ridges on the back imprinted into her fingers. She kept inching forward in the car, knowing the people behind her were aggravated and frustrated.

And then the house was before her. Her chest squeezed. *Lord, why do You keep bringing me past here?*

The Hinkley family's raised ranch faced the cor-

ner of Red Rock Road, flanking the sign that marked
the entrance to the Wildway Subdivision. Bright yellow, friendly, with big windows and a welcoming
front porch that was often dusted with snow. Julia
tried to avert her gaze, tried not to look at the twin
white-barn-door entrance to the garage, but it was
too late. Then the image blurred before her eyes.

She pulled over to the side of the road, ignoring
the irritated honks behind her, and thrust the car into
Park just as the tears in her eyes crested. Grief and
regret expanded in her chest, pushing at the walls
she'd put in place six months ago, demanding she
address the emotions. But they were too big, too
powerful and full of too many questions and doubts.

*It's your fault. You spent all that time with him.
You should have noticed something. Said something.*
Done *something.*

"I'm sorry," she whispered at the house, at the broken family inside, at a God who she was sure was
shaking His head at her inaction, until her tears ebbed
enough for her to brush them away. The Hinkleys
owned the store beside the coffee shop, but rarely
worked the shop themselves anymore. Seeing the
shop was hard, but driving past the house where Julia
had worked with their son, Darryl, laughed with his
family and where Darryl had ultimately chosen to end
his life was a whole other level of hard.

Julia shifted the car into Drive and headed toward
downtown, pushing the image of the empty porch
and the garage doors aside. By the time she pulled
in front of Three Sisters Grindhouse, she had com-

partmentalized all of it into dark closets in the back of her mind.

As she stepped out of the car, she heard the wail of fire sirens, followed by the whoops of police cars, a continuous keening that carried on the wind. Oh no. Not another one. She prayed it was something other than yet one more arson in their small town.

Chloe was wiping the counters when Julia walked in. A few regulars, college students who came in for a study group, were sitting at a center table, and their resident writer was sitting on the leather love seat in the back with his laptop open, typing away. All was quiet and normal in the coffee shop, exactly as it should be for late afternoon on a weekday. In here, it was as if the scary world outside didn't exist. Julia loved this little coffee-scented haven. Almost as much as she loved her youngest sister.

Petite, blonde and eight months pregnant, Chloe had the friendly smile and wide eyes of Amanda Seyfried. "Hey, sis." Chloe brushed an errant strand of hair off her face. "Just in time. My doctor's appointment is in twenty minutes."

"Sorry. I meant to be here earlier, but I took a wrong turn." It was much more than that, but telling Chloe meant a conversation Julia didn't want to have. Julia normally worked Mondays, Wednesdays, Fridays and every other weekend. The downtown shop was only open on Saturday mornings, which gave Chloe—who worked too hard and too much—a nice break, but left Julia with empty hours that left her mind circling a past she couldn't change. Today, she'd volunteered to come in for the last couple hours the shop was open to do cleanup while Chloe got her weekly ob/gyn checkup. Anything to get out of the house and, most of all, out of her own mind. Every time Julia tried to pick up more hours, Chloe would shut her down, telling Julia her purpose in life wasn't to make cappuccinos.

Chloe stowed the spray bottle of cleaning solution under the sink and tossed the dirty rag into the hamper by the door to the small kitchen. "No problem. All I'm doing these days is waiting for this little bean to grow." She patted her belly, then ducked into the kitchen and retrieved her coat and purse. She shrugged into the thick wool jacket and buttoned the front, then laid a hand over Julia's. "I know you're going through a hard time, Jules. It'll be okay. No one blames you."

*Except me.* "Yeah, I know." Julia worked a smile to her face, but it felt flat. "You should get out of here. It started snowing, so be careful driving."

"Yes, Mom." Chloe grinned, then swooped her long hair up and into a hat. Calling Julia *Mom* was a long-standing joke between the two of them. After their parents got divorced when Chloe was thirteen and Julia was eighteen, their mother had worked two jobs to support her kids, leaving Julia in charge more often than not. She'd become a de facto mother for Chloe, who had done her level best to rebel every day for a long time.

Their father, an airline pilot, had traveled more than he'd been home in Denver. When the girls were adults, Mom took a job in Chicago, where the winters were colder but the pay was better. In the years since, Chloe and Julia had grown even closer. Mia, their other sister, was off doing her own thing. She'd always been more of a free spirit than homebody Chloe. She'd been part of the initial investment for the coffee shop when they bought it from their grandmother, but had never had much interest in working it.

Julia grabbed one of the dark brown-and-pink aprons off the hook by the kitchen and slipped it over her head. Three Sisters Grindhouse was embroidered over the front pocket in a happy curlicue script that didn't reflect Julia's current mood. "Is Bob going with you to the doctor?"

Chloe shook her head. "He's got something at work."

"Clo, this is your first baby. He's only gone to one doctor's appointment. He should be there for you."

"He's working a lot, that's all." Chloe looked down, searching in her bag for her keys and avoiding the conversation. "After that, he's leaving town again for a conference. He's super busy, Jules."

Julia didn't say anything. She liked Bob, but he'd been distracted and absent the last few months, and as much as she didn't agree, it wasn't her marriage, and wasn't her place. Chloe and Bob had married young, when Chloe was barely twenty, and sometimes Julia wondered if maybe they hadn't learned those necessary relationship skills to keep a marriage going. The stress of the baby coming had only seemed to compound their issues. Still, most days Chloe glowed with happiness. Maybe it was just a little road bump as they adjusted to the idea of a new baby.

The bell over the door jingled, and a tall, ridiculously handsome man with dark hair ducked inside, followed by a little brunette girl with a look of complete irritation on her face. They paused in the entryway to sweep the coating of snow off their coats. He looked familiar, this lanky man wearing blue jeans and a checked button-down shirt under his open camel-colored Carhartt jacket. Then again, most of Crooked Valley came into Three Sisters Grindhouse at one time or another so she'd undoubtedly served him a latte or something.

No, not a latte, or a cappuccino or any of the froufrou drinks they had on the menu. This guy, with his dark, neat, trim hair and deep eyes, looked like a black coffee, straight-up, no-frills kind of guy.

"That's Mike Byrne," Chloe whispered. "And he's single, in case you didn't know."

It took a second to make the connection, to put the Byrne last name with the sign she passed on her way to work almost every single day. The town vet. With his daughter, given how closely the little girl resembled him—save for the scowl. Julia looked around for Chloe, but her clever sister was already waving goodbye and heading out to the parking lot with a grin on her face. Chloe, the only Beaumont sister who still believed in happily-ever-after. Julia kept the eye roll to herself, then flashed her best customer service smile at Mike. "Can I help you?"

"A hot cocoa for my daughter, Ginny, please"—he gave her an offhand, almost shy flicker of a smile— "and a few minutes of your time, Miss Beaumont."

Was that some kind of pickup line? If so, the guy must be desperate or blind because A.) she didn't know him at all; B.) she'd worn no makeup and thrown her wild mane of dirty-blond hair into a messy ponytail; and C.) anyone who knew Julia would also know she avoided dates with strangers like the plague.

"One hot cocoa coming up." Maybe if she ignored the second half of his sentence, he'd get the hint.

She filled a stainless-steel jug with cold milk, added a thin metal thermometer then stuck it under the steaming wand, angling the container at the same time she moved it in a circular pattern. The steaming wand bubbled into the milk, heating it to a few degrees shy of the normal hundred and twenty-two for a latte. She poured it into a mug with some sweetened cocoa, then added a dollop of whipped cream. "Here you go, sweetie. Hot chocolate that's not too hot, so you can drink it right away."

The little girl scrambled onto one of the stools. She cupped her right hand around the mug. The other sat in a sling, casted against what had probably been a break. Judging by the scuffed edges of the bright pink cast, the break had happened at least a couple weeks ago, maybe more than a month.

Mike put a hand on his daughter's just as she was starting to sip. "What do you say?"

Ginny cast a hooded glance in Julia's direction. "T'anks."

"You're welcome, sweetie." Julia gave the girl a smile.

The resident writer got up from his laptop, picked up the remote control and turned on the wall-mounted television that sat over the far end of the counter. Normally, Julia kept it on a music station. He glanced at Julia, his finger poised over the controller. "Okay if I watch the news for a sec?"

Julia nodded. "Sure, but keep the volume down." She gestured in Ginny's direction.

As the customer flipped through the channels, Julia shifted her attention to the vet. He was one handsome man yet he seemed completely unaware of his effect on a woman. "Do you want some coffee, too, sir?"

"Only a conversation, please." Mike nodded toward the end of the counter.

Julia cast one last glance at the girl and then stepped to the end. In the background, she could hear the low drone of the television newscaster talking about the fire that had just happened. She glanced at the television screen, and saw the scrolling headlines: *Sixth fire this year... Suspect still at large... whereabouts unknown... Fire nearly under control.*

A shiver of dread ran down Julia's spine, but she brushed it off. It was the storm and the route she'd taken and this vet who was pestering her. That was all.

Julia glanced back at her customer and nodded

toward Ginny. The customer gave her a sheepish apology before switching the news off. "Sorry. I just… Every time I hear the sirens, I get spooked," the writer said.

"We all do," Julia said softly. "Thank you for turning the television off so we don't upset anyone else." The writer nodded, gave Ginny a small smile and then went back to his table.

Julia swiveled toward the veterinarian and lowered her voice. "If this is a weird way to ask someone out—"

"I need assistance with my daughter. She's struggling because of her broken wrist, and I am not making much progress in helping her adjust. Don Conley said you were the woman to contact."

Don Conley, the elementary school principal. Nice guy, dedicated to the kids in town. She'd worked with his sister's son a year or so ago, and every time she turned around, Don was throwing her name out, like a one-man PR campaign. "Well, Don was wrong. I don't work with kids anymore."

Clearly, this good-looking guy with the easy smile wasn't used to people turning him down. He stared at her. Blinked twice. Stumbled over his words. "I, uh, was under the impression you were an occupational therapist for children."

"I am." She shook her head. "I mean, I was." Past history that did not need explaining. She thought of the front porch, empty and still now, the garage doors closed against a tragedy no one could believe, and the sad, devastated family that was inside that yellow ranch. "Now, if there isn't anything else, Dr. Byrne, the hot cocoa will be $2.49. Cash or credit?"

He slid a five-dollar bill over to her. "Keep the change."

It was a ridiculously generous tip but telling him so would only prolong a conversation she didn't want to have. Julia thanked him, paid the bill in the register then tucked the rest into the tips jar. Mike sat on the stool beside his daughter, worry knotting the space between his brows. Ginny sipped at her cocoa, taking her time and doing her level best to ignore her father.

Mike glanced around the shop while Julia kept herself busy with tidying the countertop that Chloe had already tidied. The only sounds in the room were Ginny's slurps and the easy-listening alternative music on the sound system. The resident writer came up and poured himself a refill from the carafes at the end of the counter, and the trio of college students traipsed out the door, leaving the shop mostly empty. For the first half of the day, the shop was busy, ebbing and flowing in waves of millennials and baby boomers.

"Nice paintings," Mike said, jerking her attention back to him and the daughter who was taking an interminable amount of time drinking a hot cocoa. "Who painted them?" He pointed at the pictures that ringed the top of the coffee shop's walls. Mostly done in primary colors, they were bright, happy visions of trees and fish, houses and lakes, families and pets.

Among those colorful works was one lone painting filled with dark colors and storm clouds. It hung there as a daily reminder of the mistakes Julia had made. On the rare occasions she passed that porch and those garage doors she was reminded of how horribly she had failed.

"It's the work of some of the kids I worked with. In the past." The last three words added in an emphatic point.

But Mike Byrne, clueless man, didn't get the hint. Again. "And they painted them because…?"

"It's good therapy. They don't even realize they're doing therapy when you hand them a brush and a palette. And I find that kids will talk more, deal with their fears and doubts and pains, if they're busy doing something they like." The words spilled out of her, because she'd said them a hundred times before. Before…everything.

"Spoken like a truly good occupational therapist," he said.

She shot him a glare. "*Former* occupational therapist."

Mike drummed his fingers on the counter. His gaze skipped over the couches, the chessboards awaiting players, the empty tables ready for tomorrow morning's rush. "You know this is a small town, right?"

"Lived here all my life. It hasn't exactly exploded in population."

"Which means there are no other truly good occupational therapists available locally." He put up a hand to cut off her protest. "I checked."

"That's too bad. Maybe Denver—"

"Do you know why people bring their pets to me? It's not necessarily because I'm the best vet in the state."

The deft change of subject didn't fool her for a second. "If this is some way of saying that it's all about relationships or some other customer service baloney, I don't want to hear it. I'm not taking on any new clients. Not now, not in the future."

"Because of what happened with that kid."

The sentence hit her like a slap. She recoiled and drew in a sharp breath. "He wasn't just *that kid*," she whispered, then shook her head. "I…I need to do something out back."

Julia spun on her heel, tossed the rag into the hamper then jetted into the small kitchen. She held her tears in check, kept everything behind that crumbling mental wall, until the swinging door stopped ticktocking and settled into the pocket of the jamb.

# Chapter Three

Reason number seven hundred and fifty-two why Mike Byrne avoided human beings as much as possible—if there was a wrong thing to say, he said it. If there was a feeling to hurt, he hurt it. And if there was a way to drive someone out of the room to avoid a conversation, he used it.

Whatever he had said to Julia Beaumont had been the wrong thing. He was pretty sure those words fell somewhere in between *I need help* and *what happened to that kid*.

*That kid* was a teenager who had committed suicide several months ago. When Mike asked around about Julia at the office, Keesha told him that she'd read in the paper that Julia had been working with Darryl Hinkley for three months, after the teenager crashed his car in a drunk-driving accident and shattered both his right arm and his pelvis. The accident had also killed one of his friends. Darryl had lost his girlfriend, lost his football scholarship and lost his spirit. He'd looked at months in a cast, months of rehab, a football career over before it started and, for a while, a very likely jail sentence before a judge decided to be lenient with the teenager and clear him of wrongdoing, giving Darryl a second chance at life. However, despite all the therapy and hard work, Darryl ended up killing himself. Hanged himself in the garage, Keesha had said.

That had to have been devastating for Julia. She wasn't a psychiatrist; surely she had to know she wasn't the reason. But given how much work she had done with kids in the past and judging by the number of paintings hanging on the wall, she undoubtedly shouldered a lot of the blame, right or wrong.

Mike Byrne, of all the people in the world, knew what it was like to blame yourself for the death of another. To live with guilt that lay as heavy as an anvil on his shoulders. To lie in bed on a cold winter morning and wish it had been you instead.

Why on earth had he brought that kid up? What was wrong with him? It had to be the most insensitive thing he'd ever said. Definitely ranked in the top ten. From the time he was young, his mother had told him, "Maybe there's a reason God made you so good with animals."

And that was exactly why he should stay in the exam rooms and not venture out into the real world. If not for Ginny, Mike wouldn't have left his house for anything other than work after Mary died. When her mother passed away, Ginny was four and a half and needed him to be a grown-up who could make breakfast, lunch and dinner, and wash the clothes once in a while. For weeks, he'd been incapable of more. Even now, he struggled to build a bond with his daughter. That had been Mary's department, and she'd been a heck of a good mom. For the ten thousandth time, Mike questioned the irony of a universe that took Mary away and left him to flounder along as half a parent.

"Daddy? I want a cookie, too," Ginny said. She had a ring of hot chocolate above her lip and a little whipped cream on her thumb.

In the three hours since Mike picked Ginny up at school, brought her back to the clinic and stuck her in his office to work on her reading, she'd spoken three sentences total to him. Most days, their conversations were short and stilted: *How was school? Fine. What do you want for dinner? Pizza. Did you clean your room? Yes.*

After that, Mike had exhausted his repertoire of conversation starters with a six-year-old who resented him for not being able to give her the one thing she wanted—her mother back. And, he was sure, she missed the easy family they used to have, the dad who would laugh every day, who engaged with his family. Losing Mary had made him withdraw in a way that he knew had confused Ginny. So he gave her everything else he could and prayed that, one day, it would be enough. Ginny wanted a cookie, and a cookie he would provide. That he could do. The rest? Not so much.

"All right. A cookie is fine. Let me ask Miss Beaumont when she comes back."

Ginny buried her face in the mug again. "She doesn't like you." Spoken into the ceramic interior, the words sounded hollow.

Mike turned back. "What gives you that impression?"

"She gave you the eye. Mommy used to do that when I got in trouble."

"That she did," Mike said, and the shared memory filled the space between them for a fleeting moment. He could just see Mary, one brow arched, a half smile on her face, looking at Ginny, and saying something like, *I think my very sweet daughter has been replaced by an alien, maybe a monkey...or a kangaroo?* Whatever it took to defuse the tension while teaching a lesson. As a mother, Mary had been perfect. Had more patience than anyone he knew, a knack for turning a piece of string and a crayon into an afternoon of crafts, and a never-empty heart that showered their little girl with love.

"I want a cookie *now*, Daddy." Ginny crossed her arms over her chest. "I'm hungry!"

Mike could see a selection of baked goods in the glass case underneath the counter. Muffins, cookies, little breads and some scones. He had forgotten to bring lunch to the office—again—and Ginny had ended up with a yogurt he found in the fridge and part of Keesha's turkey sandwich. Failing at fatherhood—he was doing it so often, he could teach a course.

"We need to wait—"

"I don't wanna wait! I wanna cookie!" Ginny glared at him. "You said you'd give me something to eat and all I had was that yucky sandwich."

"I'll go…uh, find one." Anything that would lower the rising volume in Ginny's words, the reminder that he was breaking promises big and small, left and right. *Mommy's going to be all right, I promise.*

That was the one he couldn't put back together. The words that haunted his nights and squeezed the breath out of him every time he saw a tear in Ginny's eyes. The least he could do was get her a cookie.

He slipped behind the counter of the coffee shop, then knocked on the door to the kitchen, which was silly, because it was a swinging door and knocking pushed it open. "Uh, Julia?" Wait. That was too casual. "Miss Beaumont?" Was she a miss? A missus? A miz?

She had her back to him, hunched into herself. He heard her take a breath. "I'll be out in a sec."

"I want to apologize. I'm…I'm an idiot, and I shouldn't have mentioned Darryl." She flinched at the name, and he realized he'd made mistake number seven hundred and fifty-three. If only life was a golf game and he could just call it a mulligan and be granted a do-over. "I'm sorry. I'm not good with people. Give me a golden retriever and I can talk for hours, but a human being…"

She turned to him. Tears filled her eyes, and her cheeks were flushed, but she brushed them off and reached past him to pull a bag of coffee beans off the shelf. "I'm not so good with people either these days."

He slipped the rest of the way into the kitchen. The door swung back and forth for a moment, then settled in place. He glanced over his shoulder and saw through the tiny window that Ginny was buried in her mug again, on the other side of the thick door. "Listen, I know you said you don't work with kids anymore, but Ginny is…she's…well, she's lost. And I'm not doing the best job at helping her get back on track. Which is why I need help."

"I'm sorry. I'm not working in therapy anymore." As Julia reached for a second bag of beans, Mike took the first one from her, falling into the pattern of a partner as easily as slipping on socks. He helped her gather two gallons of milk and a box of sweetener, taking each of the things as she put them in his arms. "What about her mother?" Julia asked. "Isn't she helping?"

"She died over a year and a half ago." The words hung in the air, heavy as storm clouds. It had gotten easier to speak them, and Mike wondered what that said about him as a widower. Did it mean he had stopped caring? Or that he'd accepted the loss? Or that he was just a terrible husband?

"Oh." Julia's face reddened. She reached for a container of muffins. "I'm sorry."

Mike scoffed, reaching for the box and stacking it on top of the pile in his arms. "I hear those words so often, and I know people mean well, but what are they sorry for? It wasn't their wife. Their mother.

They don't have to try to explain to an angry six-year-old why her mother will never, ever again bake cookies with her or help her pick out a dress or read her *Horton Hears a Who!*" His throat clogged and his voice cracked. "That's more words than I've spoken to a person in months."

"I get that." Julia's features softened. She put a hand on his arm, a light, quick touch over as fast as it began, but in that instant there was true sympathy, warm comfort. Connection. "The kids I used to work with would talk all through therapy sometimes. It was as if having to squeeze a ball or button a shirt—just something to keep their hands and brains busy—kept them occupied enough to open up."

He looked down at the pile of supplies he was holding. "There might be something to that theory."

Julia let out a laugh. "You may be right, Dr. Byrne."

It was a short laugh, a moment of détente and lightness, but Mike would take it. He could use a lot more moments like that. They all could. And there was something about this woman that gave him an ease he rarely felt around anyone. Like he didn't need to be charming or witty or social. He could just…be. Even if that being came with saying the worst possible thing. Twice. "Mike, please."

She met his gaze. Her eyes were a deep green, flecked with brown, like the far depths of a wooded lake. For a second, he felt as if he could drown right there. "Mike."

Mike cleared his throat. "Well, I didn't come back here to pester you about working with Ginny. I meant to ask you if I could buy a cookie or something for her."

"Oh, sure, sure." Julia bumped the swinging door with her hip and stepped into the shop again. "Hey, Ginny. What kind of cookie do you like? Chocolate chip? Sugar? Peanut butter?"

"Peanut butter, please."

Well, at least Ginny used manners with other people, Mike thought. He missed his daughter—the laughing, hurried little girl who had rushed through the house as if it was one giant adventure park, ready to be explored and shared. Someday, maybe both of them would find a way back to being some kind of a normal family.

"Peanut butter cookies are my favorite, too. Don't tell anyone, but I eat way more of them than I should." With a pair of tongs, Julia grabbed a cookie from the case, put it on a plate then slid that over to Ginny. "Refill on the hot cocoa?"

Ginny nodded. "Yes, please."

"Coming right up." Julia took the mug and repeated the process from before. The rich scent of chocolate filled the air. "Not too hot again."

"T'ank you." She gave Julia a rare smile. A twinge of envy flickered in Mike's chest.

"You're welcome, Ginny." Julia smiled back, and that twinge flickered again. "My new peanut butter cookie friend."

Ginny grinned a chocolate-ringed smile, then she broke off a bit of her cookie. "Want some?"

"Don't mind if I do." Julia took the crumb and popped it in her mouth. "Now, we're best friends."

Ginny giggled. She looked up at Julia with a look that was part awe, part adoration. And that envy flared again inside of Mike.

He needed to get a grip. He had no reason to be envious that Ginny was happy, for goodness' sake. Or that his daughter had had a rare moment of laughter. Or that Julia had given Ginny a smile that he wanted to see for him. What was wrong with him?

He tugged out his wallet, if only to have something to do that didn't involve staring at his daughter and this strange but beautiful woman. "How much do I owe you?"

Julia waved it off. "On the house." She wiped an invisible spot off the counter, then shot a glance at Mike. Like her touch a moment earlier, their gazes connected, and he swore he felt a bridge build between them. "It's the least I can do."

"I appreciate it. This town could use something to smile about rather than…" He let the sentence trail off instead of mentioning the arsonist and the sense of fear and dread that filled pretty much every resident of Crooked Valley.

"On that, we can agree, Dr. Byrne," she said with a smile.

Instead of money, he tugged a business card out of his wallet, plucked a pen out of the coffee-bean-filled holder by the register and scribbled his cell and his address on the back. "If you change your mind…"

"I won't."

"I wish you would." Mike left the card on the counter, then he bent and picked up Ginny's coat from where it had fallen on the floor. "Come on, Gin. Time to go home."

Julia looked at the name on the card for a long time after Mike Byrne left. Maybe she should…

No. Getting involved in the personal lives of the people she helped was what had ruined everything. She couldn't risk that again. Ginny Byrne needed more than occupational therapy—she needed a counselor. An expert in grief.

As for Ginny's father…well, he'd been something else. Tall, dark, quiet then a rush of words that receded like an angry tide. In that moment in the pantry, she'd had a picture of a domesticated life with a man who chatted about the day's events while the two of them chopped peppers and seared steaks.

Thinking about him was an exercise in futility, and Julia wasn't the kind of woman who wasted hours of her day. So she pushed Mike Byrne out of her head and set to work scrubbing down the machines and shelves, even though she'd done that yesterday, too. The business card sat on the counter, a bright rectangle against the dark granite.

Just as it was getting dark, Julia flipped the sign on the shop to Closed, more than an hour after normal closing time. She was outside, about to lock up when she saw a figure emerge from the store next door and cross the parking lot toward Julia.

Darryl's mother was a slight woman who had only

gotten thinner after the past year. She and her husband owned Daisy Blue, a clothing boutique next door, but in the past year, Julia had rarely seen either one of them there. Today, Sheila Hinkley had her dark brown hair pulled back with a clip, and a bare minimum of makeup on her face. "Can we talk?"

"Hi, Sheila," Julia said. Everything inside her ached to hug this grieving mother, but instead, she hung back in the awkward pause. Guilt was a stone in her gut, heavy and impossible. "Um, do you want to come inside?"

"Yes, please."

Julia opened the door, then locked it behind them. Even though the sign said Closed, that didn't mean a customer wouldn't try to come in for a late-day cup of coffee. Whatever Sheila wanted to talk about seemed serious, and Julia didn't want the interruption, although a part of her wished she could avoid a conversation that was undoubtedly going to be tough. Julia hadn't seen Sheila since the funeral, where both of the Hinkleys refused to talk to her. Julia had avoided them ever since, which at the very least made her a coward. "Do you want something to drink?"

"No, thank you." Sheila gestured toward a small table. "Mind if I sit?"

"Of course. Make yourself at home."

Sheila scoffed as she pulled out a chair and took a seat. "That's what I said to you when you first came to our house. Do you remember?"

Julia did. She'd been so nervous that day, knowing that Darryl had enormous challenges to overcome. He was, without a doubt, the toughest case she had faced so far in her career. Sheila must have read that about Julia and immediately set her at ease. "You welcomed me into your home, even with all you were going through," Julia said. "I don't think I ever said thank you."

"Well, it's what you do for people." Sheila sat stiff and straight in the chair, her hands in her lap. "I didn't come here for conversation."

"That's okay. I—"

"I have to admit that I've been struggling to forgive you for a long time." Her words were measured, hesitant. "You spent so much time with Darryl and encouraged him to talk about his feelings in that art you had him do, and you never said a word to us."

"I didn't know, Sheila. If I had, I would have—"

"I'm so tired of the would-haves and should-haves!" She shot out of the seat, her grief still so raw, and crossed to the paintings that hung on the wall. She pointed to Darryl's artwork. "I don't want this hanging in your shop anymore."

"Yes, of course. It should be yours. I just didn't know whether to give it to you or just wait or…" When Sheila didn't respond, Julia stopped talking. She dragged a chair over to the wall, then stood on her tiptoes and unclipped Darryl's painting from the string. "Here you are."

Sheila took it with a nod, holding the charcoal image of her late son's depression gently against her chest. "Thank you."

There was nothing to thank Julia for. She had failed at her job. Let Darryl down. "I'm sorry."

Sheila didn't acknowledge the apology. She turned away and headed for the door. She stopped when she reached it and turned back. "Did he say anything, when he made this?"

"He told me that he was struggling to forgive himself for what happened." Julia stepped forward and pointed at the drawing. "May I?"

Sheila hesitated a second before turning the picture around. Julia traced above the trees Darryl had created. She could still see him with the charcoals, sketching fast and furious. Julia had been so delighted that day because it was the first time Darryl had engaged and talked to her. All the times before that, he'd been sullen and silent, refusing to do any OT. "He said that he and his dad used to hunt in these woods. He was small, and he remembered the trees were so tall and dark."

"They'd go early in the morning, sometimes before the sun rose," Sheila said softly. "They never really shot anything. I think they just liked the father-son time, hanging out in the tree stand up on Mount Pine."

"I asked him about the shadows and darkness, and he said that the days after the accident had felt like those woods, dark and foreboding. He was facing so many uphill battles—court, recovery, forgiveness—and he didn't see a way out. But that day"—Julia drew in a breath and felt the sting of tears in her eyes—"that day he said he did. He said he was be-ginning to see how things could be different."

After that, Darryl had begun to respond and work with his physical therapist and with Julia. He'd started walking soon after that and had talked about return-ing to school, maybe even someday playing football again. He smiled, he joked—in short, he was a nor-mal kid every time Julia saw him.

Until the day he took his life.

"Maybe the way he saw out wasn't what you thought he meant, Miss Beaumont." Sheila's eyes filled with tears. "And maybe you should have said something."

She left the coffee shop and headed out into the night. Julia stayed for a long time, wishing she could do all of it over again. Wishing she could say some-thing that would ease the Hinkley family's pain, and hopefully, someday, find a way to forgive herself for letting Darryl slip through the cracks.

A little after five, she gathered her things and went home to an empty apartment. Perhaps she should get a dog or something, because the small space seemed to echo with loneliness, and tonight, the last thing she wanted to be alone with was her own thoughts. But the idea of getting a dog led to thoughts of bringing it to a vet, which led her straight back to Mike Byrne, in a vicious circle.

Just as she was digging through the freezer, hop-ing to find a frozen dinner amid the ice trays and freezer-burned mystery packets, her phone rang, and Chloe's face lit up the screen. For a moment, Julia put aside her regrets and guilt and focused on her little sister and her niece- or nephew-to-be, since neither Chloe nor her husband wanted to know what they were having. There was nothing Julia could do about the past, except try to be better in the future. "Hey, sis. How did the doctor visit go?"

"Fine. The little bean is growing into a watermelon." Chloe laughed. "Or at least that's what it feels like."

"Are you sure you don't want to cut back your hours at the shop?" Julia asked. "I don't want you to get too tired."

"And what will I do if I don't go to work? I have no knitting skills, you know."

Chloe loved working in the coffee shop. All three girls had spent most of their childhoods there working with their grandmother, but Chloe was there the most. Maybe it was because she was the youngest, or maybe because she had lived and breathed Three Sisters Grindhouse from the day she was old enough to walk.

Mia had, too. But then Mia had left for New York, leaving the coffee shop, the town and her family in the rearview mirror. She'd kept in touch off and on over the years, more off than on. Wherever their middle sister was now, it wasn't here, when they could all use her help.

"I would be happy to pick up more hours," Julia said. If only because working gave her less time to think and dwell on things she couldn't undo. Eventually, the cut in her income by stopping her OT practice was going to need to be replaced.

"Maybe after the baby comes. For now, I'm doing good. And you, my sister, shouldn't be pouring all your energies into serving coffee when you have a gift for working with children."

It was a familiar argument. "Clo, you need the help, especially as you get closer to delivering. You're going to want time with the baby after he or she arrives. That's what I'm there to do."

"No, Jules. We have part-time employees and if need be, we'll hire someone full-time so that you can go back to occupational therapy." A pause, then Chloe changed the topic. "So how did it go with Mr. Handsome Vet?"

"Mr. Handsome Vet?"

"Don't play dumb. You know you thought Mike Byrne was handsome. And he's single."

"You told me that already, Miss Matchmaker. He wasn't there to ask me out anyway. He wanted to hire me."

"To work with his daughter?" A pause. "I saw her cast. You know, Jules, that might be good for you. Get involved again, take some baby steps—"

"No."

Chloe sighed. "Julia, you are great at your job. You can't quit."

"I'm happy at the coffee shop." She said it so quick the words ran together in one fast blurred sentence.

"Are you?" Chloe asked.

Julia didn't answer. Instead, she changed the subject and made up a reason to get off the phone. That was easier than explaining to Chloe why she had no intentions of ever working with another child. If someone else's kid ended up like Darryl—

No. The risk was too great. God had sent her a huge reminder of that when Sheila Hinkley stopped in tonight.

Julia's steps seemed to echo as she crossed the kitchen, pulled open the fridge and realized she had nothing to eat except a head of lettuce that should have been thrown out last week and a quarter gallon of milk. A couple cans of beans and a box of instant mashed potatoes that looked old enough to be left over from World War II in the cabinet. She could go out—again—but her streamlined budget, now that she'd stopped taking therapy appointments, couldn't bear the weight of too many restaurant dinners. And the apartment that had seemed cozy and quaint when she bought it two years ago now felt vast, empty and cold.

Flurries danced in the breeze. Julia pulled on a winter coat, shoved her hands in some gloves then added a pair of fleece-lined boots to keep out the cold. She drove back down the hill and pulled into the lot of the small grocery store that sat at the eastern end of Main Street.

Mac's Market had been there as long as Julia could remember. Family run, like the coffee shop, it stayed small and local, carrying fruits and vegetables grown in the area, honey produced by nearby beekeepers and poultry from a free-range farm a few miles away. Steve and Jean MacDonald ran it together, with their kids working as cashiers, and from time to time their grandson came in and helped restock shelves.

Julia grabbed a cart, shrugged out of her coat and tucked it in the basket, then headed inside the market. It was edging toward six-thirty, and only a few stragglers were shopping. Most everyone else had figured out dinner and were home with their families, sitting around the dining room table, cracking jokes while they passed the peas and potatoes.

It was times like this when Julia missed being married. She didn't miss Brian at all—as soon as she'd discovered the cheating, she had erased him from her heart. He didn't deserve any space inside her brain or her emotions. But she did miss the partner part of being married. Buying for two. Coming home to someone. Having a person to talk to in the early-morning hours. The first year or so of their marriage had been like that, then he'd become distant and cold, and everything she loved about their relationship slowly dissolved. By the time she'd found out about the other women, whatever love she'd had when she'd married Brian had already died.

In the freezer section, Julia selected three microwave dinners and tossed them in the cart. If anything said pathetic and single, a bunch of three-minute spaghetti with turkey meatballs did. She turned toward the dairy section and stopped when she saw Mike Byrne and his daughter at the end of aisle seven.

Ginny was standing beside a half-filled cart with

her arms crossed over her chest. Mike had a box of cereal in each hand, and frustration etched into every corner of his face. "You like both of these, Gin. Pick one."

"I don't like those! I don't want them!"

Mike let out a long breath, then straightened. "Fine. We'll have eggs for breakfast."

"I don't want eggs!" Ginny stayed put when Mike started pushing the cart toward the milk. "I don't wanna shop anymore."

He turned back. "I'm not leaving you in the middle of the market. We are out of food, and we need to buy some." He took Ginny's hand. "Now, come on. The faster we do this, the faster we are done."

Ginny held her ground and leaned back, further cementing her position. "I don't wanna. You're so mean, Daddy. I hate you!"

A shadow washed over Mike's face, and the frustration yielded to a deep, deep hurt. Julia knew that look. Knew what it felt like to be butting your head against a wall, trying so hard to do what was right, only to fail time and time again. "Listen, Ginny. If we can—"

"No!" Her scream hit decibels that only dogs could hear. A couple shoppers turned to look at them and shoot Mike bad-parent glares.

Julia rolled her cart up to sit beside Mike's. Not because she was getting involved, not at all. Just helping defuse a situation. Nothing more. "Hey, Ginny. Nice to see you again."

"Hi." Her voice was low and sad, her gaze on her toes.

Julia bent down, to reach Ginny's level. Tears stained the girl's flushed cheeks, and her arm hung in the sling, heavy and limp. "I'm sure it's hard to eat cereal and eggs with only one arm, huh?"

Ginny nodded. "Cuz that's my arm I use all the time."

"You're a leftie. Like me." Julia gave her a smile. "Most people are righties, and they forget about us lefties. You know, when I broke my arm, my mom made me pancakes and muffins. They were much easier to eat with my other hand. Do you want me to ask your dad if he can do that?"

Ginny nodded again, harder this time. "I like pancakes."

"Me, too, especially with blueberries in them." She got to her feet, then turned to Mike. Even with the thick camel-colored coat over his button-down shirt and jeans, he could have been an ad for a cowboy, all lean and rangy and heart-stoppingly handsome. "It's about the cast, you know, not the Cheerios."

"I didn't even think of that." He shook his head, and his face fell. "I'm not good at this single-parent thing."

"Don't beat yourself up. It's hard sometimes to see the world from the viewpoint of someone who is hurt. Just keep her broken wing in mind when you're picking out things to eat. A fork is tough to manage with your nondominant hand."

"I should have known that. I've just been…"

"Distracted. I get that." She gave him a smile, if only because it felt right. Not because she was hoping he would return it with one of his, thus far, rare smiles.

"Yeah." He cleared his throat. No smile. "Well, thanks."

"Anytime." It was an offhand word that people threw out all the time, but when she saw a light in Mike's eyes, she realized he thought she meant she'd changed her mind about working with Ginny. She was only helping him with a kiddie meltdown and adding a little more kindness to a town that had been on a razor's edge for months, nothing more. "If I see you around, I mean."

"Yeah. If." He gave her a disappointed nod. "You have a good evening."

"You, too." As Mike walked away, with Ginny keeping pace beside him, Julia took a quick scan of his cart. A half dozen microwave meals sat in the basket, along with ready-made snacks and already chopped apples. They could have had twin sad-life grocery bills.

What would it be like to sit down at a table with him? To have a dinner that didn't come out of a box and have a conversation that didn't center around Guatemalan beans versus Colombian beans? Or worse, another silent meal all alone?

She shook her head and swung her cart in the opposite direction of Mike Byrne. That kind of thinking was what got a woman into trouble. Especially a woman who made it a rule to never, ever get involved again.

As Julia unloaded her groceries onto the conveyor belt, she noticed a rack of fire extinguishers and dead-bolt locks where the gum and candy bars should be. "This is new," she said to the cashier, a young girl of maybe seventeen.

"And apparently necessary," the girl said. "My manager said people are buying extras so he put some in here. I heard the hardware store sold out of extinguishers because the businesses around here are all spooked. That last fire was pretty close to here."

"Let's hope they catch whoever is doing this soon." Julia took a last glance at the locks and extinguishers, a scary sight in a family-run grocery store. "Very soon."

## *Chapter Four*

The high noon sun cast the entire front porch with a dark shadow, making it look more like a bear's den than a home. Cal Moretti, Mike's best friend from high school, sat in a scarred old kitchen chair, peeling peanuts and tossing the shells into an empty coffee can. Cal had settled in Crooked Valley after he'd returned from his last tour. Most of Cal's family had either died or moved and when he'd told Mike that a quiet, easy life was what he needed after those years of war, Mike had helped Cal find a house in town.

Cal tossed another shell toward the can and it dropped to the bottom with a soft clink.

"If only footballs were as easy to aim as peanut shells," Mike said as he strolled up the walkway. He'd opted to get a fast-food burger for his lunch today so he could spend his lunch hour convincing Cal to create the harness system for Scotty.

Cal jerked his head up. A smile spread across his

bearded face. "Depends on who's catching it—or not catching it."

"The sun was in my eyes that day."

"Heard that excuse. Don't believe it, butterfingers." He got to his feet and clasped Mike's hand with both his own. Cal was a tall man, over six foot, with broad shoulders and powerful arms. He'd added a few pounds since his high school days but still managed to make men half his age look on in envy when Cal was lying on that bench press, thrusting heavy plates into the air like they were cotton swabs.

The missed pass during the homecoming game fifteen years ago was a familiar debate they'd had dozens of times since those high school days. Every time, it was like easing back into their friendship, even though the military and veterinary school had taken them on divergent paths. "Got a minute?" Mike asked.

"Sure." Cal patted a second empty chair beside him. The chair had seen better days and looked about ready to collapse. Mike passed on the seat. "You want a soda or anything?" Cal asked.

"Nah. Heading back to work in a few." He pulled a sheet of paper out of his pocket and unfolded it. "I need you to make me something."

"What on earth is that supposed to be a drawing of?"

"A doggy wheelchair, essentially." He pointed out the frame, then the wheels. "I have a corgi patient that's having trouble getting around because of his degenerative myelopathy."

Cal arched a brow. "Really, Einstein? With the big words again?"

Mike rolled his eyes. "Okay, in *layman's* terms, the dog needs a wheelchair that can support his back half while his front half is zipping along."

"I don't think I can do this." Cal studied the sketch. "Looks kinda specialized."

"It is. But I found a lot of great websites with information on how to create one. And I have all the measurements for the dog right here." He pulled out the rest of the papers in his pocket—a set of images from websites that made this kind of thing, the details of Scotty's body size and even a how-to Mike had found on a DIY site.

Before the war, Cal had been a genius, creating custom machines for shops all around the country. Needed a machine that could bend a steel box, stamp it with a design and weld it shut? Cal was the man to go to. He had loved the puzzle of inventions, the challenge to create something no one else could. In the military, he'd been a munitions expert, one of the best with handling the intricacies of bombs. Then he'd gotten injured, and he'd stopped caring about puzzles and challenges.

Since then, he'd been in trouble off and on with the Crooked Valley Police Department, usually when his misery and his temper got the best of him. He'd spent a few weeks one summer a couple years ago working with teenagers at a ranger-type camp, something Mike thought would help Cal find his center again, but all the experience seemed to do was remind him of what he had lost when that blast went off.

Cal kept telling Mike he'd get back on track soon, but sitting on his porch stewing all day wasn't the path to living a normal life again. Hence the project and a way to give Cal something constructive to do. Something that reminded him he could still work and have meaning in his life.

The chair creaked as Cal leaned back. When he was sitting down and wearing jeans, no one could see the shrapnel scars on his leg, the caved-in muscles eaten away by compartment syndrome after the surgery, the curve of the metal leg that replaced the lower half he'd lost. Or the mental scars that kept him out on this porch, shelling peanuts while the day passed. "You should order one or something. I make machines, Mike. Not wheelchairs for dogs."

"This isn't really for the dog." Mike caught Cal's gaze. "It's for Henry Rathburn, whose dog is declining. Henry isn't ready to give up on him yet. And frankly, neither am I."

Cal scrubbed his chin with one hand, studying the sketch and the measurements. "Henry Rathburn, huh?"

"Yeah."

"Kid lives right down the street."

"I know."

"You tugging on my heartstrings, Byrne? Because I'll have you know I'm not a softie."

Mike draped an arm over the back of the chair. "Of course not. You're a big, mean, strong marine and QB. Ain't nobody gonna call you a softie."

"That's right." Cal grinned. "Man, you are a pain in my neck, you know that? Every time I turn around, it's *Hey, build this, Cal,* or *Fix this.*"

That was true. Mike had been on his doorstep at least once a week for six months. Of the requests Mike made, Cal turned down nine out of ten, but Mike kept coming back, sometimes inventing things he needed—like a spice rack for spices he didn't use—just to get Cal out of that chair and out of the endless loop of regret and anger in his head. "Keeps you out of trouble, though, doesn't it?"

"Some people might agree." Cal looked at the drawings again and let out a long, heavy sigh. For a second, Mike thought he was going to say no again. Instead, he gave Mike a small nod, then he stuffed the papers into his shirt pocket. "I'll come up with something in the next day or two. Might need to order some parts—"

"They'll be delivered by five today." Mike had decided he would convince Cal, no matter what it took, even if it meant dropping a box of supplies on his porch.

A smirk took over Cal's face. "You were that sure I'd say yes?"

"You never let me down, not once, on the field, Cal. You were there when my parents got divorced, and you were there when…" Even now, he had trouble talking about it. "Anyway, I've always been able to count on you."

"Not everyone thinks that, you know." Neither one of them needed to mention the brushes with the law and the reputation for being a troublemaker that Cal had garnered as a result.

"Not everyone knows you like I do." He leaned over and clapped Cal on the shoulder. Their gazes met, and years of friendship and support formed the cement of their bond. Then Mike quirked one side of his mouth. "And for the record, it was the pass that was bad. Not the catch."

"Keep on telling yourself that, butterfingers," Cal called after him as Mike headed toward his car. "If it helps you sleep at night."

"Keeping you busy helps me sleep at night," Mike said under his breath as he slipped back into his car. Cal had already left the porch, leaving the chair and the unshelled peanuts behind to head for his workshop out back. For a moment, the world of Crooked Valley seemed normal, then a chill cut through the air and reminded Mike that there were bad things brewing in the shadows.

Mike stared at the clock on his dashboard. He had thirty minutes until his next appointment. There was paperwork and lab results waiting for him at work, an endless stream of phone calls and emails to return, but instead of heading for the clinic, he was sitting in a parking lot, telling himself he really needed a cup of coffee.

In the distance it took to cross from the parking lot

to the door of the coffee shop, Mike had convinced himself that yesterday had been a fluke. That flicker of attraction he'd felt for Julia Beaumont was due to stress or lack of lunch. He was sure she wasn't as mesmerizing as he'd thought.

But then he opened the door, stepped inside and she was there, and his pulse tripped. She was handing a mug to a customer sitting at the counter, laughing at something the customer had said. She had a nice laugh, reminding him of the wind chimes that had hung in his grandmother's garden and tinkled a soft melody on stormy nights.

What was wrong with him? He didn't get romantic or think about melodies and tinkling music. He was cut, dried, to the point. No poems about roses or eye color. He'd been brought up in a tough, rule-filled household where crying was for sissies, and emotions were weaknesses. He'd learned to keep his head buried in his books and his brain focused on facts. Mary had known that going into their marriage, although she teased him about being so uptight she could stick a pin in him and he'd deflate.

Julia glanced up, and the smile on her lips died. Probably because he was starting to look like a stalker. Ginny was still in school for another few hours, and Mike prayed with everything he had that she stayed there today. No getting in trouble, no scuffles on the playground, no trip to the principal's office.

"Dr. Byrne! So nice to see you!" Harriet Nichols came up to him, her hand out in greeting. He'd been so distracted by Julia he hadn't even noticed Harriet coming toward him. A short woman with a ring of gray curls and a fondness for pink lipstick, Harriet had been in the office a few times. She was a kind woman with a soft voice who owned a couple of cats that were her pride and joy, and regularly spoiled.

"Afternoon, Mrs. Nichols."

"You come to the Grindhouse? I don't think I've ever seen you here." She took his hand and half led him up to the counter. "I'm here most afternoons, don't you know, getting a little midday pick-me-up and a little distraction from the news of the day. All that business about arson... It's got me as jittery as a bird in a thunderstorm. That's another reason why I'm drinking half-caf nowadays. Well, that and because my tummy isn't a big fan of caffeine. Getting old is tough. That reminds me, I need to bring Delilah's kittens in to get their vaccinations. I'll call your office in the morning and make an appointment."

All Mike could do was nod and make a vague noise of agreement because Julia had smiled at him and he lost his entire train of thought.

"Hi, Harriet. I have your usual all ready," Julia said, sliding a mug across the counter. "And, Dr. Byrne, what can I get you?"

"Just coffee, thanks."

"Well, you certainly came to the right place for that." She grinned, then pulled a vanilla-colored mug off the shelf. "Latte? Cappuccino? Espresso?"

He could see why Harriet liked the coffee shop. It was like an oasis, not just from the ordinary stresses of life, but from the constant worry everyone had about the arsonist running around town. Inside this quaint shop, that world ceased to exist and became one where neighbors hung over the fence and chatted away an afternoon. "Nothing fancy, just black."

"That's what I thought," Julia said, her voice so low he almost didn't hear her. A smile ghosted on her face, then disappeared.

Harriet pulled a five-dollar bill out of her purse and pushed it toward Julia. "Put that on my tab, please. And, Dr. Byrne, don't you argue with me about it. You've been a great vet to Samson and Delilah."

Mike gave her a nod. "Thank you, ma'am."

Harriet blushed at the chivalry. "It's nothing. Have a good day, Dr. Byrne. I'll leave Julia to entertain you now." Harriet picked up her coffee and crossed to one of the tufted love seats where another woman about Harriet's age waited.

"So...do you sing songs?" Mike asked Julia.

She spun around. "What?"

"Sing songs. Or maybe dance?" His conversational skills were so bad he needed a remedial course in small talk and making jokes.

Her brow arched, then she rolled her eyes. "Please tell me that wasn't a joke about me entertaining you."

He'd been trying to get her to smile, the way she had smiled at Ginny, but his utter lack of social skills meant he couldn't even pull off a joke. He shifted his weight. "Guess it's a good thing I'm a veterinarian and not a comedian."

"Yes, good thing." But she chuckled under her breath. Okay. That was a great sign. If dorky humor was the secret to getting Julia Beaumont's attention, Mike had plenty in the vault. Especially given how pretty she looked today, with her hair up in a clip and a dusting of bangs across her forehead.

"So tell me the truth," she said as she handed him a mug of a rich, dark brew. "You're not just here for the best cup of coffee in Colorado, are you?"

"No. I'm here to plead my case again." No sense in lying. All that did was skirt the issue, and Mike had done enough of that since he lost Mary.

"You're determined, I'll give you that." She leaned against the wall and crossed her arms over her chest. The towel dangled from one hand. She stood there a moment, thinking, and Mike let the moment pass. He wasn't the kind of guy who had the urge to fill space in a conversation. "I'm not working as an occupational therapist anymore."

"As you have previously told me."

"But…" She tipped her head, studying him. Her green eyes seemed to go on forever. "I suppose I could meet with Ginny and then give you a referral for someone who would be a good fit for her."

It wasn't a yes, and it wasn't an answer, but it was one move closer to both. And there was some irrational side of him that was also pleased that he had an excuse—no, valid reason—to see her again. "That would be great."

She pulled out her phone and opened her calendar

app. "When would you like to schedule the meeting?"

"Tonight." He put up a hand before she disagreed. He didn't want some impersonal evaluation in his office or some other sterile location. Ginny had been through enough of that kind of thing. So had he. Plus, this whole excuse—*valid reason*—to see her again could be a chance to repay the favor, and given what he'd seen in her grocery basket the other night, this was a favor he could easily make happen. "I don't know about you, but it's been a long time since I've had a meal that didn't come out of the microwave. Why don't you come for dinner tonight, say around six? It's the least I can do to repay you."

"You cook?"

"No, but it's been said I'm exceedingly good at takeout." He gave her a grin that hopefully said, *I might not have a lot of people skills but I'm harmless and know the best place to get pad thai.*

She laughed then, a deep, genuine laugh that seemed to bubble up from some well inside her and spill into the room. A laugh that Mike Byrne liked very, very much. Maybe too much. "Takeout, it is, then. See you tonight, Dr. Byrne."

"Tonight." He gave her a nod, then headed for the door. A smile landed on his face and stayed there long after he got back to the office.

The standoff started at 5:45. Ginny stood in the kitchen, one fist on her hip and a determined line to her mouth. "I don't wanna."

"Gin, you need a bath." It had been his bright idea to let Ginny go out in the yard when they got home. He'd forgotten that it had rained earlier today, turning yesterday's snowfall into slush, and by the time he saw the mud, it was too late. "You got all dirty from playing outside and—"

"I don't care. I don't wanna."

He leaned toward his mud-spattered daughter. Dark splotches covered every inch of her, from her ankles to the top of her head. Her face had a dusting of mud freckles, and her brunette waves had specks of dirt on the ends. She'd left her shoes in the back hall, but the rest of her looked like the aftermath of a tropical storm. "Let me just put the bag on your cast—"

"I don't wanna! You can't make me!" She took off like a jet, running down the hall and into her room. The slam of the door made for some strong punctuation.

Mike balled up the plastic bag, tossed it to the side then leaned against the counter and let out a sigh. Across from him, a trio of pictures of Mary sat on the top of the island in little silver frames. Mary holding a newborn Ginny; Mary kneeling behind Ginny and grinning with their twin cat costumes for a party; Mary holding out a birthday cake, the candles flickering a soft glow on her features, while Ginny drew in a deep breath and prepared to blow them out.

In every single picture, Mary was smiling. Ginny was smiling. And Mike—well, he was either behind the camera or at work. He wasn't the one who knew how to swaddle or craft or bake. He'd been the provider, the bedtime enforcer, the tall shoulders at the town carnival. Mary had been the life and spark in their family, and he was, he supposed, the muscle. Or at least that was how it had seemed…before. Everything before was different from now. Every single thing.

He ran a hand over his face. "How'd you do it?" he asked her picture. Mary, with her deep brown hair and her wide green eyes and smile that went on forever, didn't answer, and knowing she never would nearly broke his heart.

Either way, he still had a bath to give. An evening to salvage. An attitude to change in the next fourteen— no, twelve—minutes. "Ginny—"

"No!" came the emphatic shout from her room.

He picked up the plastic bag and roll of tape again and headed down the hallway. "We need—"

The doorbell rang—a welcome interruption to a battle that Mike was pretty sure would last until bedtime. The dinner delivery. Thank goodness. He pivoted, dropped the bag and tape on the hall table then crossed to the tiny foyer. Behind the hazy image created by the beveled glass, he saw a familiar head of honey-colored hair. Not the teenager from the Thai place, after all (a kid Mike knew so well he might as well have adopted him into the family, given how often he ordered takeout), but the intense and beautiful Julia Beaumont.

"You're just in time," he said as he opened the

door. "Giving a bath around here is like negotiating a hostage crisis."

She laughed. "Well, at this age, kids like to start testing their boundaries. Trying to be a little independent."

He liked her laugh. Very much. "I think Ginny is filling out a lease agreement as we speak."

Julia cocked her head. "Did you just make a joke?" She smiled. "Good. Keep on doing that." Then she brushed past him and into his house, leaving Mike wondering who was in charge here, because it sure wasn't him.

And that might not be such a bad thing.

Five feet inside Mike Byrne's house, Julia could see why the man had such a problem connecting with a six-year-old. Every square inch of the house was as pristine as a military barracks. The floors gleamed, the windows sparkled, the pillows marched down the sofa in coral-white-coral-white precision. Not a single dish sat on the kitchen counters, and the laundry room she passed didn't have so much as a stray sock in the color-coded hampers for sorting. And most of all, there wasn't a single toy or book or stuffed animal lying around.

She doubted he was a bad dad, just an overwhelmed one who had poured all his efforts into cleanliness and order because the rest of his home life seemed to be a chaotic disaster. Add in a six year-old girl with a broken wrist and a bad attitude, and it was no wonder Mike came looking for her.

Didn't mean she was the right one for the job—but she'd get him connected with someone who would be great with Ginny and that would be enough. She could pull Mike Byrne and his daughter out of the Guilty Feelings part of her brain. And maybe then she wouldn't keep thinking about him, because that's all she'd done since that moment in the pantry.

It had seemed so normal, working together, talking. No, more than normal—comfortable. As if they'd been partners forever. She'd never known that ease with Brian, or anyone else for that matter. Maybe it was because he was a vet, and a gentle spirit came with the job description. Whatever the reason, she'd thought about him a dozen times since this afternoon.

"So, where do you want to talk?" She pulled a list out of the back pocket of her jeans, bringing both of them back to the subject at hand. All business. No personal. "I brought a list of therapists—"

"Daddy! I need help!" Ginny's voice carried down the hall. At the same time, a small rusty sedan pulled into the driveway. A plastic sign reading Tasty Thai was mounted on the roof. Mike peeked out the window. The driver honked and waved at Mike.

She could see the immediate war in Mike's eyes—pay the delivery guy or help his daughter. "You take care of him," she said. "I'll go check on Ginny."

"What if—"

"I've got it under control." She stood there for a second. "Uh…which way?"

Mike stepped back and pointed, just as the delivery guy parked. "Down the hall. Second door on the right."

"Got it." Julia dropped her coat and purse on the bench by the door, then headed down the hallway.

He and his daughter lived in a split-bedroom one-story ranch, with a bath and two bedrooms on one side, and a master on the other. Every inch of the house was neat and tidy, as organized as a Marie Kondo convention. A handful of framed pictures on the plain cream-colored walls, no knickknacks collecting dust on a hall table.

No pets, either, which seemed odd to Julia. Didn't most vets have like five dogs and a bunch of rescue cats? Before she could wonder why, she reminded herself that she wasn't getting involved.

And knocking on his daughter's bedroom door wasn't getting involved?

It was helping out. Being a good neighbor. Julia rapped three times. "Ginny? It's Julia Beaumont from the coffee shop. Your dad asked me if I could help you while he paid the delivery guy."

"I made a mess."

Julia took that as assent and turned the knob. She poked her head inside Ginny's room or, rather, into an explosion of pink and white, with a giant four-poster bed, a squat double dresser and a fort in the corner decorated with mosquito netting and pink bows. "Are you…oh my."

A puddle of water was gradually spreading from

the attached bathroom and into Ginny's room, like a slow tide reaching across the sand. Ginny stood there, clutching a well-loved teddy bear, a somber, regretful knit in her brows. "I was trying to take a bath. Cuz Daddy got mad at me. Cuz I was dirty."

"Gotcha." Julia bit back a laugh, then she scooted into the room, sidestepped the water that was only a couple inches away from the thick white shag area rug and hopscotched into the bathroom and over to the tap. She turned it off and plunged a hand into the tub to pull the stopper. Water began gurgling down the drain. "Crisis averted. Let's get this cleaned up."

"Daddy's gonna be mad." Ginny looked down at the spreading puddle on the tile floor. Maybe a quarter inch deep, the bulk of the water had been held back from the bedroom by a wooden threshold. Thank goodness.

"He's going to be proud that you tried to take a bath all by yourself. But maybe"—Julia reached out and touched the cast—"wait to do these things until you're all healed. Okay?"

Ginny's mouth twisted. "I gotta use a bag. Cuz I'm not s'posed to get my arm wet."

Julia bent down. The kid sure was a mess, as if she'd rolled in a pigsty. "I can help you with the bag when you take your bath. Then while you're getting all nice and clean"—Julia tapped a finger on the muddy dot on Ginny's nose—"your daddy and I can clean up the water. Sound like a plan?"

Ginny nodded.

Julia looked at the giant puddle on the bathroom floor. Nothing a couple dozen towels couldn't handle. "Ginny, why don't you get your pajamas so you can put them on right after the bath?"

"So's I won't get cold."

"Exactly." When the little girl ran into her room, Julia reached across the puddle and grabbed a stack of towels off the rack against the wall. Two more tumbled onto the floor, landing in the worst of the water. Julia laid two towels across the floor to form a path to the tub and then began mopping it up, one towel in each hand, pushing the water back into the bathroom.

Ginny came back and stood on the edge of a towel, her bare toes curling against the water. "Can I help? Cuz then Daddy won't be mad at me. I promise to take my bath right after."

The overfilled tub had drained quite a bit and would need to be refilled with some hot water anyway. Plus, allowing Ginny to help cleanup gave her some ownership in the disaster, a good lesson to learn. "You sure can. Here you go." Julia plugged the drain again, then handed Ginny a towel and showed her how to blot the water from the tile floor. "Watch your cast. Don't get it wet."

"What on earth happened here?" Mike's irritated voice cut through the room. "Ginny…"

"Sorry, Daddy. I was trying to take a bath and—"

Mike let out a gust of emotion. "Ginny, you made a giant mess!"

Julia got to her feet and pressed a fresh towel into Mike's arms. "She knows that. And it's just water. I told her we would clean it up while she gets a nice, warm, bubbly bath."

"But she should—"

"Chill out a bit. It's just water," Julia repeated. "It won't hurt anything."

Mike's dark brown eyes met hers, then flicked to a very contrite Ginny, standing beside Julia with a damp towel in her hands. The irritation faded, a little at a time. The stress in his features melted.

"You're right," he said softly, then he bent down to his daughter. "Why don't you let us clean the water up, Gin? You go get the bag for me to put on your arm and then you can have your bath."

"With bubbles?" A hopeful lilt ended Ginny's words.

"Sure. As long as you promise to keep them all in the tub this time." He ruffled her hair, then sent her to get the plastic cover. When Ginny was gone, he turned to Julia. "Thank you."

"I didn't do much. Just put down some towels—"

"You did more than you know. If it had been me handling this, Ginny would have had a meltdown and we both would have ended up going to bed early." He gave her a smile. "That was another joke, by the way."

She'd been so caught in his smile that she barely heard the words. "Oh yeah. Ha."

"Okay, let's see if we can get Lake Superior mopped up." Mike glanced at the mess, drew in a deep breath then kicked off his shoes. Barefoot, he walked across the bathroom, set the tub to refill and poured in a healthy dose of bubble bath. On his way back, he grabbed more towels and tossed a couple to Julia. "Not how I planned on spending this evening. Or utilizing your time. I apologize."

The dark green towel beneath her palms grew even darker as it soaked in what looked like a gallon of water. "It's okay. Puddles happen."

He grinned at that. "By the way, I ordered pad thai, and I probably should have asked if you liked Thai food first, so if you don't, let me know. I'll grab a pizza. I don't have soda, but I do have tea and coffee that I can make. I wasn't sure what you liked and…" He shook his head. "For the record, I stink at this."

"You're doing fine." The nerves were actually a little endearing. It was as if they were in high school and he was rambling around, trying to find the right sentence to ask her to prom. "And I love coffee, as I'm sure you know."

"Oh…oh yeah." He shook his head. "Sorry. Me, too, but I like my coffee plain. And…you knew that already."

"I knew you were a black coffee kind of guy the first time you walked in. Straight, no frills, neat and easy."

He chuckled. "You just described my entire life."

She grinned at him as she traded the sopping towel for the next one in her stack. Together, they managed to get the bulk of the water off the floor. He turned off the tap and helped Ginny into the tub. The bubbles made her giggle and forget all about the inconvenience of her arm.

Mike and Julia stood in the doorway, him leaning against it. The floor was dry, the bubbles plentiful and some kind of soft rock station played on the radio in the other room. Ginny laughed and talked to her toys and thoroughly enjoyed her bath. The love Mike had for his daughter shone in his eyes, but it was clouded by the frustration of the chasm between them.

"I realized something today," he said after a long while. "It's about the bubbles, not the mess."

Julia crossed her arms and pressed her back to the wall. "What do you mean?"

"Back in the store last night, you told me it was about the cast, not the Cheerios. I've been thinking about that ever since." He pivoted, and his attention focused entirely on Julia. "Maybe I'm looking at things all wrong."

"Go easy on yourself. You're a single dad with a busy job. It's understandable."

"Maybe for other single parents, but not for me." His gaze went back to his daughter, and to someplace far, far from this room, these bubbles and this moment. "I have to get this right," he said with a soft, burning fierceness in his voice. "I'm all Ginny has. And I can't…"

His voice trailed off. The only sound was the splashing coming from the tub. "Can't what?"

"Can't let her down again." In his eyes, she saw a vulnerable man who was scared to death of screwing up. A man so far from shore he was going to need a lighthouse to get back. "I just don't know how to do that."

"I don't know if I know how anymore either, Mike."

"You seemed to do pretty good here." He made a sweeping gesture of the small bathroom. "The mess is nearly gone."

"It was only water."

"Maybe to you." He picked up a pile of wet towels and dumped them in the hamper. "It was a lot more to me."

She saw the trust and hope in his eyes, and she backed away. "It was just water, Mike. Nothing more. Please don't read anything into a few towels on the floor."

"I don't mean to pressure you," he said. He took a deep breath, and seemed to do a mental reboot of the conversation. "I'll drop the subject and the only thing we'll discuss is the correct level of spiciness in Thai food."

When Julia had agreed to dinner earlier today, she hadn't expected this man and his struggling daughter to touch her heart. She shouldn't get deeper involved with this family. She'd already decided she wasn't going to work with Ginny, so really, Julia could just leave the list with Mike and be on her way. But then her stomach rumbled and her feet didn't seem to want to move. "Since Thai is my favorite kind of food, you have an unfair advantage." She smiled, and when he smiled back, it felt as if the world was settling back into the right orbit again.

They were just sitting down to eat when the sound of sirens began to fill the air, cutting through the valley with their sharp, insistent notes. Mike's and Julia's gazes met, both of them saying the same thing: *not another one*.

This fire would be number seven. How long would it be before the police caught the arsonist and the people of Crooked Valley could rest easy again? Every time she heard the sirens, Julia was reminded that this town she loved wasn't the same, not anymore. She thought of the fire extinguishers and the locks at the grocery store, which was only a couple blocks from the coffee shop. Two of the fires had been downtown. Were other businesses at risk?

Like hers?

"Daddy, the fire trucks are so loud." Ginny covered her ears and made a face.

"They are," Mike agreed. His face filled with concern as he listened. "They sound like they're…"

"Downtown," Julia finished on a whisper. Just as she said that, her phone buzzed. She fished it out of her pocket and saw Chloe's name on the screen.

There's a fire in the shop next door. I'm afraid the coffee shop will be next.

That was all it took to get Julia out of her seat and rushing out the door, pulling on her coat as she dashed for her car, whispering prayers that her pregnant sister was far, far from the coffee shop right now, safe at home.

## Chapter Five

It took a solid three minutes to convince Chloe to leave. She stood in the back of the coffee shop, clutching a gift bag to her chest, as stubborn as only a little sister could be, refusing to abandon Three Sisters Grindhouse, even as tendrils of smoke began to creep under the doors. Twenty yards away the fire department had just arrived. Firefighters had fanned out, setting up equipment, going door-to-door to evacuate anyone inside nearby shops. They'd argued with Chloe, and when she refused to go, Julia offered to intervene. But the blaze that had started in the Daisy Blue clothing shop grew every second they remained where they were, and Julia was barely holding back the fear nipping at her heels with every puff of smoke. "Chloe, the longer you stay here, the more danger you are in. Please, let's go."

"But this is our family shop," Chloe said. "What if it catches on fire? What are we going to do?"

"We aren't going to do anything, Chloe. The firemen will put the fire out. And if it reaches our shop, I'd rather have you alive than some building." Julia shoved Chloe's coat into her arms. "Either you leave now, or I'll carry you out."

Chloe covered a cough with her elbow and nodded. Her eyes had started watering, and clearly she could see that staying was foolish. "Okay."

"Thank goodness. Come on, let's go." They hurried out the back door of Three Sisters Grindhouse, sending a grateful wave toward the fireman who was on his way to evacuate them. Chloe and Julia came around to the street side of the shop and crossed to where other shop owners were huddled in a small, tight circle, watching the firefighters pour water on the flames. Several cars and a dark pickup truck were parked in the lot across from the fire. So many people, so grief-stricken by another one of their own being attacked by the arsonist. What had started out as a vague threat in other parts of Crooked Valley was now very close to home. Too close.

The clothing store, owned by the Hinkley family, was only separated from the coffee shop by a small parking lot. The thought that the arsonist might have been targeting Three Sisters, too, nagged at Julia. There was no one she knew who hated the Hinkleys or Julia's family that much, though. Why would anyone hurt so many small businesses and private citizens?

When Julia first arrived, the fire was small, contained in the back corner of the wooden structure, but even as the firefighters began their battle, the flames grew, fed by gusts of wind, sending the fire crawling up the side of the frame and onto the roof.

"They've already gone through so much," Julia said to her sister. "Why would God deliver another loss to the Hinkley family?"

"I don't know, sis." Chloe wrapped her arms around Julia. "I don't know."

It took another half hour before the fire was brought under control and finally doused, but the damage had been done. Half of the store was completely gone, and the rest, a charred skeleton of what it used to be. Only the eastern wall remained intact, looking as if nothing had happened. There were murmurs among the other owners, everyone wondering why the arsonist had targeted another building downtown and, most of all, why he had yet to be caught.

Jimmy Long, a firefighter that Julia had known for years, trudged across the street. "Can I talk to you two for a minute?"

"Sure." Julia put an arm over Chloe's shoulders, and they walked away from the group. "Thank you for putting that out before it reached our shop."

He nodded, then lowered his voice. "Listen, I probably shouldn't be telling you this, but I heard the arson investigator talking. They think the fire might have been meant for your shop, too."

Julia's heart clenched. And to think Chloe was right there, in the middle of it all. If something had happened to Chloe... "Our shop? But why? How?"

"I don't know. The only thing that saved your store was being uphill from Daisy Blue." Jimmy pointed toward the western corner, the first part to go up in flames. "There's a trail of gasoline from the corner of your building to this one. We think the arsonist was trying to knock two birds out with one stone. He set the fire here, then ran down to the other shop, spilling some of the gas as he did. What he didn't count on was the wind and the hill. A big gust of wind must have come along and pushed the incendiary device down the hill, and the flames followed, hitting Daisy Blue instead. You two are very, very lucky."

"Oh my goodness. I can't believe how close we came to losing everything," Chloe said.

Julia clutched her sister's hand, so grateful that she had gotten her out of there and that a gust of wind had saved them. "Why were you even inside, Chloe?" Julia asked. "The shop has been closed for hours."

"I came back here because I'd forgotten something at work. And when I was unlocking the door, I…" Chloe glanced at Julia, then Jimmy. "I saw someone in the shadows, but I didn't think anything of it. This is Crooked Valley, you know?"

The implied sentence: *nothing bad ever happens in Crooked Valley*, but Julia knew the truth: bad things, tragic things, happened all the time.

"The investigator is going to want to talk to the both of you," Jimmy said, "but if I were you, I'd stay far from here for a long, long time. Until we catch this…animal, no one is safe in this town. And clearly, none of the businesses are, either."

A car rushed into the parking lot. Bob slammed the sedan into Park, then scrambled out of the car and over to Chloe. He grabbed her in a tight hug, then looked her over, his face etched with concern. "Oh, Chloe. Are you all right? I left the conference as soon as you texted. I'm so sorry I wasn't home, honey. Are you sure you're okay?"

"I'm fine, Bob. Just a little shook up. The fire never reached the shop."

"You shouldn't have come back here. Especially not at night and not without me because..." He looked at the dripping building across from them, charred black and a total loss. A heavy cloud of despair hung in the air. Seven fires in the last few months. Little by little their beloved town was being torched, eaten away by flames and anger. "Crooked Valley isn't safe anymore."

After he put Ginny to bed, Mike paced his living room, waiting for Julia to text or call. As soon as she'd told him about Chloe's text, he'd been worried that Julia would end up hurt trying to rescue her shop or her sister. He flipped on the news and found a live report on a local television station about the fire. The camera showed the view of the little store next door to Julia's. The building was clearly a total loss.

Another one and, this time, much closer to people he cared about. His practice was only a couple blocks away. Was the arsonist picking off the downtown businesses one by one? When was this going to stop?

As the reporter started to speak, the cameraman zoomed out, and Mike could see the coffee shop had been unscathed. That meant Julia was probably just fine. Still, it didn't curb his worry, and when she replied to his text a few minutes later, enormous relief flooded him.

I'm safe. Chloe is a little shook up. Rain check on our dinner?

Sure. We can talk tomorrow. He paused, then added, And I promise to pay you in Thai food.

She replied with a smiley face. Come by the coffee shop after work? The shop will be closed. I'm just going to do some cleanup inside.

See you then.

He held his phone for a couple more minutes, hoping to see three dots appear, followed by another text, but there was nothing. That made sense, because there really wasn't anything else he needed to settle with Julia Beaumont right now. But for some reason, he missed her cheery demeanor and her smile more than he expected. She'd brought a lightness to what could have been a tough situation tonight with Ginny by putting everyone at ease, which, in turn, eased Mike's stress. It had been a long time since he'd felt peace like that.

He packed a healthy portion of the leftover Thai food into two plastic containers, one for his lunch and one to give to Julia, then went to bed. He stayed awake for a long time, staring at the ceiling, certain he could still smell smoke in the air. Danger was so close…too close.

And yet, every time he went through town, he saw

the ironic juxtaposition of hope amid the fear. Bright, happy Christmas decorations hung in the shop windows and in people's homes. A holiday that should be about joy and gratitude had been marred by the smoke and flames. This wasn't the kind of Christmas Mike wanted for his daughter. Or for anyone.

The next morning, Mike woke a grumpy Ginny up for school. She gave him a bleary-eyed glare. "Do I hafta go to school?"

"Yes. So you'll grow up to be supersmart." He perched on the edge of her bed and thought about Julia's advice the other day. Maybe it was time he changed things up, because what he was doing so far definitely wasn't working. "How about pancakes for breakfast?"

"Is it my birthday? Cuz we only have pancakes on my birthday." Ginny sat up and swung her legs over the side of the bed. Mike helped her into her robe, then put her arm back in the sling. Tomorrow the cast would be off, and Ginny could start getting back to normal, with some help from a physical therapist. Maybe they both could find some kind of new normal.

"No, Gin, it's not your birthday. We're just doing something different today." He glanced around Ginny's mess of a room, opted not to say anything during this fragile peace between them and instead crossed to the door. He paused when he heard Ginny's voice behind him.

"Daddy?" she said, waiting until he turned to look at her. "I like different."

He turned and smiled at his daughter, his heart full just looking at her wide eyes and riot of curls. "I'm glad." For the first time in a long time, Mike felt a little bit of hope that maybe, just maybe, he could get this parenting thing right.

That started with getting the pancakes right—not as easy a task as he thought. The problem with a breakfast he only made once a year was being out of practice making said breakfast. It took him two batches to get the consistency right, and three pancakes before he got the timing right and stopped burning them. By the time he finally put two pancakes on Ginny's plate, her excitement about the different breakfast had ebbed and she was once again sporting her best grumpy face. When Mike tried to brush her hair, things only got worse. Ginny started to cry when he tried to loosen a tangle, and eventually he gave up and just swooped everything into one big ponytail. "But I wanted braids," Ginny said. "Like Mommy always did."

Mike sighed. "I don't know how to do that. The ponytail is just fine. Go get your shoes on or you'll be late for school."

She pouted and turned away from him. "I wish Mommy was here. She was nicer."

Ginny barely said anything when he dropped her off at school, and Mike wished for the thousandth time that he had been blessed with the easy way that people like Julia Beaumont and his late wife had with words. They would have known how to fix this.

The workday passed in a blur of pets and owners,

topped off by Harriet Nichols coming in with Delilah's kittens, a mewling bundle ready for their first shots. "You have the necessary vaccinations at this time," Mike said to Harriet. "So if you wanted to post an adoption notice on the bulletin board, these kittens are ready to find homes."

"I can't let just anyone take Delilah's kittens," Harriet said. "I'm very choosy about who gets one of my kittens."

"I understand that, Mrs. Nichols. But there are people out there who would love to give a home to one of these cuties."

Harriet nodded. "You're right, Doc. I'm just more worried and not thinking straight with all that's going on in town. I can't believe that arsonist hit the store next to the coffee shop. It's getting so scary I don't even want to leave my house."

"I'm sure they'll catch whoever is behind this soon."

"Did you hear what the news said this morning?" Harriet asked. "They think it's someone who has some anger issues. Someone who is reclusive. Someone who is blaming the rest of the world for whatever is going on with them."

"That could be a lot of people," Mike said. He thought of Cal and all the anger his friend had brought home from the war. The little project of building a cart for Scotty was all part of Mike's way of helping Cal get back to the jovial, warm man he used to be.

Keesha poked her head into the exam room. "School's on the phone for you, Doc."

Mike sighed. "Tell them I'll be right there." He gave the kittens one last exam, then handed the rest off to Jamie and headed back to the school again.

Don Conley's voice wasn't anywhere on the scale of delighted by the time Mike got a chance to get to the school. A sullen Ginny, once again covered in scrapes and dirt, her ponytail lost somewhere along the way, leaving her hair a tangled mess, sat in the oversize chair outside the principal's office.

"I got in a fight with Becky," Ginny said. "She said I was dumb cuz I didn't do good on my spelling test."

"Didn't do *well*, Gin." Mike sighed again. "Sit there and please be good. I'll be back in a second."

This time, the principal didn't pull any punches. "I'm afraid we have a zero-tolerance fighting policy at this school. As it is, I already gave her a pass on the first fight, because we decided to call it a misunderstanding, but this was a definite fight on the playground, and I can't ignore that. Ginny has to face some kind of consequences. I understand that she's been through a lot, so why don't you just have her stay home for a few days and we'll keep this whole thing off her record? Three days of a sort-of suspension, and that includes today. That's what I told Becky's mother, too. Ginny has a lot to deal with, but we can't let her keep getting into fights."

"Three days?" Mike glanced over his shoulder. He could see the back of Ginny's head through the glass of the principal's office. Even from this angle, she looked sad and weary. "Don, I have a business. I can't just take three days off. And you know I don't have anyone else who can help me with Gin."

Don steepled his fingers. His face tightened into serious lines. "Maybe you should look at this as an opportunity, Mike. Take a little time off, spend it with your daughter. Christmas is right around the corner and then winter break. Maybe some dad and daughter time will do her some good before school starts up again."

Except Mike had no idea what to do for dad and daughter time. Ginny no longer seemed interested in playing Candy Land or coloring pictures or cuddling on the couch with a movie and some popcorn, not that he'd been there for much of that when she was little. Those things had always been Mary's department. Mary, the mother of the year, who knew just how to tease a smile out of a grumpy day or soothe a bruised knee. Mike could calm a frightened dog or a hissing cat, but when it came to human children… he was clueless. Three days—technically two and a half since today was partly over—of arguing and grumpy faces stretched before him like an eternity. What on earth would they do all day?

"I've been a principal for several years," Don said. "And I've found that a lot of kids' behavioral issues boil down to one common denominator. Granted, some have mental health issues, others have been diagnosed with ADHD or other behavioral disorders, and that is certainly a big factor in kids acting out, but that's not the case with Ginny. I'm not a doctor, but in my professional opinion, Ginny is acting out because she's still dealing with some emotional trauma from the death of her mother. In short, Mike, I think she needs you, desperately, and is trying to get your attention."

"By getting into fights? All that does is make more trouble for her."

"Young children don't have the words or understanding to express what is going on inside them. All they know is that they feel a need for your attention, and whatever gets them that is what they keep on doing."

He thought about that for a moment and saw the commonality with his own work. How many times had he had a similar conversation with a new pet owner? "Like a puppy, I suppose, in some ways. To undo negative behaviors with a dog, you give them tons and tons of positive reinforcement so that they don't feel the need to act out."

"All creatures have a need for love." Don put up a hand before Mike could get defensive. "Now, I have no doubt you love Ginny more than life itself. But she's struggling, and she needs to know that more than ever before."

Which meant Mike was falling down in the expressing his emotions department with his daughter, too. He just wasn't a warm and fuzzy, feel-good, words kind of guy, and he wasn't so sure he could learn to be anything else. When Mike had been a kid, his stern father, a soldier from the day he turned eighteen, discouraged any and all emotions, breeding into Mike a tendency to "be a man" and keep everything locked deep inside. He was too old to learn how to do things differently. "How on earth do I do that, Don? Between work and managing the house and Ginny, I barely have enough time to eat. It's been a long eighteen months."

"I have no doubt about that. And believe me, you have my sympathy. I can't even imagine how hard this has been on you and Ginny." Don drummed his fingers on the desk while he considered something. "I have an idea. My brother has a two-bedroom cabin up on Mount Pine. He lives in Arizona during the winter and gives me the keys to use the place if I want to go fishing or whatever. I was going to go this weekend, but that storm is rolling in, and I'm buried in things to do here before Christmas break. Why don't you"—Don dug in his pocket and produced a set of keys—"head on up there with Ginny?"

"The practice—"

"Work doesn't need you as much as Ginny does."

Mike knew Don was right, of course, and Mary would have said the same thing if she had been here. Ginny had been as adrift as Mike after the death of her mother, and the gap between father and daughter had only widened, not narrowed, in the last few months. His practice would survive a few days of being closed, and he could always refer any emergencies to a neighboring veterinary practice. His relationship with Ginny, however, wouldn't survive if he didn't course correct.

It was as if God was speaking directly to Mike's heart, forcing him to see all that he had ignored for so long. It was past time to set his grief and his fear of failing as a dad aside and focus solely on his daughter. Whether or not he would do things as well as Mary wasn't the point, not anymore. Ginny needed him. Simple as that. "Maybe I'll take her exploring in the woods. She might like that. And the rest… I'll figure it out as I go along."

"Sounds like a plan. There's an extra cot and all the supplies you could need up there. My brother keeps it well maintained." Don got to his feet and pressed the keys into Mike's hand. "Have a merry Christmas, Mike."

Christmas. Yet another thing he had avoided thinking about or planning for because that had always been Mary's department. He'd gotten the tree out of the box after Thanksgiving, and retrieved some of the decorations from where he stored them in the back of the office, but that was as much decorating as he'd managed.

Ginny deserved a merry Christmas, one filled with all the magic and sparkles he could muster up, especially with all the fear circulating in the air. This year, with his father's health declining, his parents had headed south for the holidays, and that meant Mike had to figure it out on his own. Sooner rather than later.

"You, too, Don. And thanks for this. I appreciate the wake-up call more than you know, as well as the chance to get out of town while that arsonist is still out there." He gave his baseball buddy a nod, then headed out of the office. "Come on, Gin, time to go home."

"Okay." Ginny gathered up her things and trudged along behind her father. "I'm in trouble, aren't I?"

"Yeah." Mike put a hand on Ginny's shoulder and gave it a pat, but she just remained stiff and unyielding. Clearly there was a big difference between deciding to change and that change actually manifesting in his connection with his little girl. Maybe he needed some reinforcements, just for today. He'd stop in and make sure Cal was doing okay, then it might be a good idea to go have a cup of coffee with someone who made his day easier to carry. "I have to run an errand, Ginny, but after I'm done, I was thinking we should go get another one of those hot chocolates."

"With Julia?" Ginny's features brightened, the difference as noticeable as turning on a light in a dark room.

He had to admit he felt that same little lilt of anticipation at seeing the occupational therapist again. There was just something…calming about her. As if being around her gave him all the answers he never had when he was alone and trying to figure out this parenting thing that seemed to come so naturally to everyone else. "Yes, with Julia. I take it you enjoy being in her presence?"

Ginny nodded. "Yup. She was super nice to me, and she helped me with my arm and my bath and everything."

This was the most animated he'd seen Ginny all day. There was clearly something magical about Julia Beaumont and her way with people—and kids. Something that Mike Byrne needed a lot more of right now. "Well, let's hope we can convince her to assist us some more," he said under his breath. "Because God knows I need the help."

Cal Moretti was waiting for him on the porch again. But this time, the army veteran seemed to be in a good mood. He was holding on to the wheelchair device he'd built for Scotty the corgi and smiling. Clearly, the project had been good for Cal's morale. Mike whispered a prayer of gratitude for the change in his good friend's demeanor.

Ginny raced up the porch stairs and plowed into Cal's side. Cal let out a loud *oomph*. "Uncle Cal! I missed you."

Some time ago, Ginny had started calling Cal *uncle*, and Mike had never corrected her. Mike's own family was small—he was an only child of two parents who had retired and traveled more than they were in Colorado—and Cal was one of his closest friends, and probably as close to a brother as Mike would ever have. Mary had been an only child as well, so when Cal returned to town from Afghanistan, wounded and deeply depressed, Mary and Mike had taken him in as one of their own family members. Mike had been there for Cal through all the surgeries and the painful process of getting back on his feet, and Cal had been there for Mike after Mary died. There were times when the trauma brought Cal down into the depths again—as had happened the last time Mike had been here—but Mike had vowed long ago to do whatever it took to keep his friend's spirits up and his faith intact.

Ginny's contagious joy and energy was clearly one of the ways to do that. Cal gave Ginny a wide, welcoming smile. As Ginny's godfather, Cal adored Ginny and spoiled her rotten every birthday and Christmas, and in turn, she brought the cranky veteran some much-needed childlike levity.

"Hey, Gin-Monster. How have you been? How's the arm?"

"It's fine. The doctor's gonna cut off the cast tomorrow. Daddy says they use a big saw but it won't hurt me cuz it doesn't have the bitey kind of teeth."

Cal chuckled. "Well, I think you are a very brave girl. And I'm very proud of you for listening to the doctor and getting better."

"Most of the time," Mike amended. Ginny had been in two scuffles at school, which were definitely not on the doctor's recommendation list. Maybe Don was right and there were some emotional issues behind Ginny's behavior. Maybe it was the frustration of the cast, or frustration with her father—or a combination of the two—that had Ginny acting out more than usual. Either way, it was good to see her happy and animated with Cal, and all the trouble from earlier today forgotten.

"What's this?" Ginny touched the canine cart and spun one of the wheels. "It looks like a race car."

"Well, it kind of is, but for a dog. I built it for your

dad so that he can help a little dog with a bad leg learn to walk again."

"Just like you. 'Cept you have a metal leg. And you don't have wheels." Ginny propped one fist on her hip and the other under her chin, studying the contraption and then her adopted uncle. "You should put wheels on your leg. Then you can go superfast."

Cal chuckled. "Maybe I should. I'm not sure if the world is ready for a superfast Cal, though."

"If anyone can make it work, it's you, my friend." Mike stepped forward and took the cart from Cal and looked it over. The craftsmanship was phenomenal, like all of Cal's work. He'd fastened PVC piping together with a supportive harness sling for the dog to wear. Two giant wheels at the back provided the locomotion Scotty was going to need. Cal had even made the height adjustable, so that Mike could fine-tune the fitting for the corgi. "This is great, Cal. It's exactly what I was looking for."

"Thanks. I enjoyed making it." His gaze went to the garage, where his workshop had resided for nearly a decade. "It was a good exercise for me, and it reminded me of what I love doing. Designing, building, solving problems. It made me consider getting into building custom things like this and maybe even some one-of-a-kind furniture."

"I think that's a great idea," Mike said. This was exactly the outcome he had hoped for when he'd given Cal the project. He'd wanted the doggy wheelchair to spark the interests that Cal had put aside when he returned from the war. "You've certainly got the talent. Lots of people in Crooked Valley would love your work."

Cal shook his head. "Not for regular people. For people with disabilities. Pieces that can make their lives easier."

"And have wheels?" Ginny piped in.

Cal chuckled and ruffled her hair. "Yes, some of the pieces will have wheels." He looked at Mike and his brow knitted in confusion. "Anyway, what are you doing here in the middle of the day? Don't you have work, and shouldn't this little monkey be in school?"

"Yes, and yes, but…" Mike lowered his voice. "A certain little monkey was suspended for three days for fighting."

Cal arched a brow in surprise. "Ginny? What's this about fighting?"

"Becky pulled my hair," Ginny said with a little pout. "And she called me stupid."

"Now why would she do that?" Cal asked. "You're the smartest girl I know."

Ginny's gaze dropped to the floor. "Cuz I don't have a mommy. Becky says that's stupid, and she says I'm stupid, too. And she said that all kids have mommies at Christmas, and I won't get any presents because I don't have one."

Cal bristled at the obvious hurt in Ginny's face. It took all Mike had to keep his own temper under control. No one had told him that Becky had said such terrible things to Ginny. His daughter had only mentioned the spelling test teasing. He had half a mind to call Becky himself and tell her to leave his little girl alone. Maybe it wouldn't hurt to make a call to Becky's mother about teaching her daughter not to be so insensitive. He hated seeing his daughter hurt, especially over something that was still so painful.

"Well, Becky is dead wrong," Cal said. "Families come in all shapes and sizes, Ginster. So that's why you got into a fight with her?"

Ginny nodded. "Becky's so mean."

"Maybe so," Mike said. A whisper of grace ran through him. Most kids didn't act out like that unless they had a reason to, and maybe Becky herself had something going on at home. Mike could understand that emotional roller coaster and the tendency to say or do the wrong thing. In the past eighteen months, he had not been his best self. Definitely not been the best father. He'd been so wrapped up in his own emotions that he'd snapped at people, been impatient with Ginny and basically been too stubborn to get out of his own way. That was going to change, Mike vowed, starting today. "Or maybe Becky is going through something herself, and she took it out on you."

Ginny considered this for a moment. "Her mommy and daddy are getting a divorce. She's kinda sad all the time cuz she might have to move."

"There you go," Cal said. "Becky was wrong for calling you stupid, but I think she also needs some grace and maybe a hug. Changes like that are really scary for kids."

"Like when my mommy died." The grief in Ginny's

voice pierced Mike's heart. How he wished he could make all this easier on his little girl. Bring some lightness into her life again this Christmas.

He thought of what Julia had said, about how he could work with a scared or angry animal and calm them easily. All it took was patience and kindness, he realized. Something he could easily give to Ginny, too.

Mike bent down to his daughter's level. "That was a tough time for you," he said. "And for me, too. I miss your mommy a lot."

"Me, too," Ginny said with a long, sad sigh.

"Well, how about tonight we look at some pictures of Mommy and I tell you some stories about her?" Mike asked. There were dozens of stories about Mary that Mike should be sharing, especially as Ginny got older. Talking about his late wife wasn't as painful now as it had been right after she died, he realized.

Ginny nodded. "Okay, Daddy. I like Mommy stories."

"See?" Cal said. "It's a good thing you have such a great daddy *and* your supercool uncle Cal to help your daddy tell only the really great stories. And I happen to think that's the smartest thing any girl could have, especially the supercool Uncle Cal part."

Mike rolled his eyes and chuckled. There were days when he was very grateful to have Cal Moretti in his life, even if he did make dorky jokes. Good friends like that were invaluable.

"I still miss my mommy, though," Ginny said. "She was the best."

Mike took Ginny's much smaller hand in his and met her gaze. "I miss her all the time, too, Ginny. And I'm sorry if I haven't talked to you about that as much as I should. It's still very difficult for me."

"It's okay, Daddy. You're sad, too."

"Yes, honey, I am." Oh, how he loved his daughter. Mike gathered Ginny into a hug and held her tight, the two of them finally building a bridge in the gulf of their grief.

Finally, she pulled away. "T'anks, Daddy. Uncle Cal, can I give you a hug, too?"

Cal chuckled. "I thought you'd never ask. I was starting to think your dad was hogging all the good hugs." He hoisted Ginny onto his knee and gave her a hug. "Promise me no more fighting?"

"I promise."

"That's a good girl." He kissed her temple, then set her down. "Why don't you go inside and see what Tank the cat is up to so I can talk to your dad for a minute?"

Ginny nodded enthusiastically. She loved Cal's overweight, slow and docile cat, who did nothing but purr and sit in the sun. "Can I give him a treat?"

"Just one. Tank's starting to look more like his namesake every day. That cat is spoiled." Cal pulled open the screen door and let Ginny in the house.

"Thank you," Mike said after his daughter was gone. "You made her feel better."

Cal shrugged. "It was nothing. You did all the hard work."

"It was huge and taught me I should maybe talk less and listen more to my kid. I don't know how you do it. Talk to kids like that and get through to them."

"I'm the cool uncle. It comes with the title." Cal grinned, then his face sobered. "Hey, I just thought I should let you know that the police and fire marshal were here today."

"What? Why?"

"They were questioning where I was last night. They think just because I did munitions in the military that makes me an arsonist."

A chill ran down Mike's spine. "Those are bombs, not fires, and besides, you're not that kind of person, Cal."

"Tell that to the Crooked Valley Police. You know Jim Daly, that defense attorney whose office got hit? He defended me one time when I got picked up for a drunk and disorderly, back when I was kind of falling apart inside." Cal's features were filled with regret and shame. "I'm just mentioning it in case you hear something about it. They want me to come in for questioning this afternoon. I heard on the news they might be bringing in some federal investigators, too."

"Do you want me to go with you?"

"Nah. I was in Afghanistan. I can handle a meeting with the cops. Besides, once they rule me out, they can move on and hopefully find whoever is doing this."

"Are you sure? Tomorrow, we're going to go up to

Mount Pine to stay at Don Conley's brother's cabin for a few days, but I can put that off," Mike said.

"No, no, go. It'll be nice for you and Ginny to get away for a bit."

Mike nodded. "We should be home Christmas Eve."

"Plenty of time to hang a stocking for me by your fireplace. Tell Santa I want a new band saw."

Mike laughed. "Yeah, I'll get right on that." He glanced at the house and saw Ginny inside on the living room floor with Tank. "I haven't done much decorating or anything for Christmas. It's just not the same without Mary."

"It never will be, Mike. You have to learn to roll with that and carve out some new memories and new ways of doing things." Cal tapped his leg. "Like I did. My life is no worse, no better, just different. I had to learn to adapt, and so do you."

"Because I'm so good at change." Mike scoffed. "You know me. I like to know what's coming from a thousand miles away, and then overprepare for it."

Until God threw a curveball in the way, and a drunk driver T-boned Mary's car and sent her crashing into a wall, throwing everything Mike knew into chaos. The steady presence in his life was suddenly gone, and he'd been forced to upend everything he knew.

But had he, really? Almost as soon as the final mourner offered their condolences and the last casserole was stowed in the fridge, Mike had slipped back into his cocoon of organization, schedules, rules and emotional distance. And look where that had gotten him—with a daughter who was still hurting and desperate for a relationship with her distant father.

"No one's good at change." Cal got to his feet and clapped Mike on the shoulder. "But you find a way to accept your losses and move on. And sometimes, you find something new that makes you happy again."

Mike thought of Julia Beaumont. Her smile. Her tender way with Ginny. Her strength. He could imagine being happy again with her in his life. He didn't know if imagining a different future—one where grief didn't hang a shadow over every minute of their lives—was a good or a bad thing, but it was something he was willing to run with and see what happened. Take a risk and step way outside his safe, predictable comfort zone, a space that almost echoed with the void of a partner, someone to journey through life with. Maybe God had brought Julia into his world to help ease him through these difficult times, or maybe He meant her to be Mike's new future. Either way, Mike was willing to see what came next. Today, he vowed, he would ask her on a date. No pressure, no expectations, just…hope.

"Hey, why don't you come up for a night or two to the cabin?" Mike said to Cal. His friend spent far too much time alone, and a few days with his favorite niece might make all the difference. "It has two bedrooms and a cot so there's plenty of room. I know Ginny would love to see more of you."

"I might just do that. I'll have to check my social

calendar, though. It's pretty full because the Cool Uncle is a popular kind of guy."

"And you're pretty full—of yourself, Mr. Cool Uncle."

Cal laughed. "Did you just make a joke?"

Mike scowled. "Why is everyone so surprised every time I do that?"

Cal gave Mike's shoulder a squeeze. "Because the Tin Man is loosening up a little bit more each day, and it's a really fine sight to see."

## Chapter Six

Bob hovered over Chloe like a worried mother hen. He'd taken the day off from work and was supposed to be doing remote work, but he'd barely left Chloe's side. "Do you have enough pillows? Do you need something to drink?"

Julia bit back a laugh at her brother-in-law's incessant worrying. Ever since the fire next door to the coffee shop, Bob had stayed close to Chloe. He'd stressed about how tired she was, if she had enough to eat, and how the baby was doing, to the point where he was clearly driving his wife crazy.

Chloe grabbed his hand. "Honey, if you put any more pillows on this couch, you won't be able to find me. And I have a seven-pound bowling ball pressing on my bladder, so the last thing I want is something else to drink. I love you, and appreciate you, but I'm fine."

"Okay." He looked a little lost for a second. "Well,

I'll just be in the kitchen working if you need anything."

"I'm fine," she said again. "Quit worrying so much."

Bob bent down and met his wife's gaze. He brushed a tendril of hair off her forehead. Everything about him softened when he looked at her. It was the kind of way every woman would want her partner to see her, and it made Julia just a little envious. For a second, she imagined Mike looking at her like that, then pushed the thought away. She and Mike weren't a couple like that. And besides, he probably wasn't even interested in her as anything other than a friend.

"I'm never going to quit worrying, Chloe," Bob said. "I've been so scared about the baby coming. About whether I'm going to be a good dad, whether I make enough to pay for a child and give him or her the life they deserve, whether I'm going to be there for you when you need me. And instead of talking to you, I buried myself in work, and I missed so much already. That fire…how close I came to losing you." He shook his head. Emotion filled his eyes, choked his voice. "I know what's important now, and I am never going to forget it."

Tears shimmered in Chloe's eyes. "I'm already a hormonal, emotional mess. It's not fair to make me cry." She gathered him in her arms and hugged Bob tight. "You're going to be the best dad ever because you're already the best husband. Now, get out of here because I think all this lovebird stuff is making Julia sick."

"I love seeing you happy, Chloe," Julia said. And she did, because her little sister deserved that happily-ever-after fairy tale. "And I would be so blessed to have someone look at me the way Bob looks at you."

The image of Mike Byrne flickered in her mind again. She had a feeling that he was a man who could love a woman with the same kind of love that Chloe and Bob had. She'd seen Mike be vulnerable, kind, even tender, when he was with his daughter and knew he was a man who loved—and loved deeply.

But he was also a widower who had clearly loved his wife very much. Was he ready to love again? Or would the next woman in his life always be in his late wife's shadow?

And was she ready to love anyone? The last time she'd gotten close to someone, the worst had happened. She didn't want to hurt another family, but most of all, she didn't want to be hurt herself. Losing Darryl had nearly broken her.

Then an arsonist had put her pregnant sister in danger, and Julia had no intentions of letting that slide, even if that meant there was a target on her back. Why the arsonist had targeted Three Sisters Grindhouse was beyond Julia, but either way, she would do what it took to keep her sister safe. Later today, she vowed to call a security company and have them install additional cameras on the building.

Hopefully that would be enough of a deterrent to keep the arsonist from going after the coffee shop again. Would he move on to another business downtown? Like Mike's veterinary practice? A shiver ran down her spine. She couldn't bear the thought of someone else she cared about being in the literal line of fire.

Cared about? Since when did she start caring about Mike Byrne?

"Julia. Hey, Julia."

Chloe's voice yanked Julia off a thought train that was pointless because there wasn't a relationship to even consider. She wasn't in love with Mike, and he wasn't in love with her. He was only seeing her because he wanted help with his daughter. Not because he was actually interested in something more. Something Julia wasn't sure she should be considering.

"Sorry, Clo. What did you say?"

"I'm worried about you being at the Grindhouse alone. I know the arsonist has never struck the same area twice, but that doesn't mean he won't come back and try to finish the job."

"I'm only going because I have to start the cleanup so we're ready to open again in a few days. I'm also going to have more security cameras installed as soon as possible so that if he does come by we'll have him on video. Besides, that arsonist is a sneaky snake who only hits at night. I promise not to stay late and be home well before dark."

Chloe gave her a dubious look. "Okay. I'm still going to worry, though."

"I'll be fine and be even more cautious than before." Even as Julia said the words, she knew Chloe had a point. Just because the arsonist hadn't come to the same place twice didn't mean he wouldn't, especially if he'd intended to burn down two businesses and only succeeded in torching one.

Chloe worried her bottom lip. "Well, if you insist on being there today, do you promise to text me every hour?"

"Of course," Julia said. "Because I'll be checking up on you and my niece-to-be."

"It's gonna be a nephew," Bob called from the kitchen.

Chloe put a protective hand on her belly and laughed. "I'm sorry, Bob, but I'm on Julia's side. I want a little girl. I'm going to buy her lots of dresses and—"

Her voice cut off when a breaking news report about the arsons came on the television. Chloe raised the volume. Julia lowered herself into an armchair, and Bob wandered in from the kitchen, the three of them silent and scared as the reporter talked about the investigation. In the background, footage from the previous fires ran on a loop, ending with the fire at Daisy Blue.

"Sources at the fire department say the arsonist is smart, well-versed in how fires work and has left very little evidence behind. There are rumors that the person doing this is former military and experienced with munitions and incendiary devices. If you have any tips, please call the tip line."

"I can't believe a former soldier would do that," Chloe whispered.

"I can't imagine anyone doing this," Julia said. "It takes a lot of hatred to try to destroy other people's livelihoods." Julia and Chloe had decided to close Three Sisters Grindhouse for a few days, but made sure to pay their two part-time employees for the missed work so at least there were two livelihoods that wouldn't suffer.

The reporter kept talking, her face serious and drawn. "The Crooked Valley Fire Department has enlisted the help of the Bureau of Alcohol, Tobacco, Firearms and Explosives to catch this predator before he strikes again. This morning, they released a sketch based on witness testimony from last night. This witness was leaving work just before six p.m. when they saw a hooded figure running through the parking lot between the Daisy Blue clothing shop and Three Sisters Grindhouse."

"Oh my goodness." Chloe put a hand to her chest. "I was there when that happened. Remember I told you I saw some guy outside? What if I missed a clue? What if I was supposed to pay better attention last night? What if he knows I saw him and he's going to come after me next?"

"They'll get him, honey. Don't worry. Until then, you'll be safe and sound with me. The coffee shop will be fine without you for a few days, and I'm going to work from home until they catch this guy." Bob sank down beside her and drew his wife into him. He pressed a kiss to the top of her head and met Julia's gaze, silently vowing to protect Chloe no matter what. Julia gave him a slight nod of agreement.

The sketch artist's drawing flashed on the screen. It wasn't much to go on—a man in his late thirties or early forties, wearing a black hooded sweatshirt. He had a close-trimmed beard and was wearing sunglasses, even though it had been pitch-dark out. The sunglasses, the newscaster said, were what caught the witness's eye. "The suspect is five foot ten or eleven, about a hundred and eighty pounds. He may have military training and is possibly armed so don't approach the suspect. If you think you have seen him, please call the Crooked Valley Fire Department. Again, do not approach this person. Let law enforcement do their job." The reporter paused. "And on a personal note, I hope they catch whoever is doing this before they terrorize Crooked Valley again."

Chloe clicked off the television. She snuggled closer to Bob, and they both put a hand on her abdomen, where their unborn child was safe and protected from the world. For now.

The heavy, acrid smell of burned wood, insulation and plastic hung in the air around the coffee shop. The charred remains of the clothing store beside Three Sisters Grindhouse formed a stark skeleton against the crisp Colorado winter sky. A sense of loss and fear hung in the air, heavy and thick.

A shiver of fear ran up Mike's spine. His practice was only a couple blocks from here. Only by the grace of God had both his business and Julia's been spared. Getting out of town and far from the danger literally knocking on their doors seemed like a very, very good idea right now. He'd shut down the practice, too, just to make sure all of his employees stayed safe.

"Daddy, was there a fire?" Ginny clutched his hand tighter. She had her favorite teddy bear tucked under her other arm. Her eyes were wide, and she was doing that thing where she gnawed on her lower lip, something she only did when she was nervous or scared.

"Yes." How he hated that there was someone in his town doing things that scared his daughter and put the residents he loved in danger. Why would anyone burn down a shop, owned by a family that had already been through too much, just before Christmas? And most of all, where was God? It was a question Mike had asked himself a thousand times since Mary died. Where was God in the midst of senseless tragedies?

His faith had been a roller coaster over the last eighteen months. Gratitude for his daughter to fill his days with meaning after losing his wife, then anger at her death. Feeling alone and adrift, without a guiding hand from above, then seeing people like Don as a nudge in the right direction.

"Did anybody get hurt?" Ginny's voice was soft, shaky.

He paused in the parking lot and bent down to face Ginny. She wanted answers, reassurance, but Mike didn't have any of those. "I don't think so. But, Ginny, you don't have to worry about that bad man because I'm right here with you and I'll protect you."

"But...but...where did the fire come from? Why did the bad man make the fire?"

"There are a number of people who would like to know that answer, Ginny." He glanced around downtown and saw another burned building a block away and a third three doors farther down. So many fires in such a short amount of time. Fires with no rhyme, no reason, just some psychopath on a rampage in the sleepy town of Crooked Valley. It was a scary time, and Mike could only pray that the fire department caught the arsonist soon. "You're safe with your daddy," he said again as he scooped her up and settled her against his hip, her stuffed bear tucked between their bodies. "Come on, let's get some hot cocoa." The arsonist only struck at night, so they should be safe at the coffee shop. Plus, Mike wanted to check on Julia, just for his own peace of mind.

"And can I get a cookie?"

He took a last glance at the building that was now in ashes, another reminder that life was short and could end in an unexpected instant. "Definitely a cookie, if Julia has any left."

Three Sisters Grindhouse was empty, with only Julia sitting at the counter, wiping a stack of mugs one by one. Even above the scent of roasted coffee beans, he could catch the acrid scent of smoke. "Mike, Ginny. Nice to see you again."

"I saw the sign said Closed. I'm glad you're shutting down." He set Ginny on one of the bar stools, then took the one beside her.

"Soon as I finish the cleaning here, I'll go home.

Even if we did open, I doubt anyone would come in. That…" She glanced at Ginny, clearly weighing what she was going to say. "Uh, what happened next door has the customers on edge."

"Daddy says there was a fire but nobody got hurt," Ginny said. "Can I have a cookie?"

"And a hot cocoa to go with that," Mike added. That was one good thing about children—their resilience and ability to bounce back from almost anything that came their way. They didn't dwell in the past or get stuck in the present like adults did. Maybe Mike should take his cues from his daughter next time, because he sure felt like he'd been stuck in mud for a very long time. "Coffee for me, please. Black."

"I know." Julia grinned. "And a cookie for you, too, Dr. Byrne?"

"Why not? It's been a day unlike any other." He realized for the first time how exhausted he felt, as if the weight of the last eighteen months had suddenly caught up with him. So many things loomed before him—Ginny's suspension, the three days his business would be closed and the impact on his bottom line, along with a holiday season he was ill-prepared to deal with. Everything needed his attention at the same time, and as much as he had vowed to move forward in a different direction than the one he'd been following for the past eighteen months, he wasn't sure he knew how to do that.

Julia poured him a cup of coffee, steamed some milk for Ginny's hot cocoa then warmed two peanut butter cookies and slid the plate across the counter.

Ginny grabbed hers and took a bite, then smiled like she'd just won the lottery.

"These are yummy. Thank you, Miss Julia."

"You're very welcome. I have lots more where those came from, by the way." She sighed and sat down across from them. "Dozens of cookies, in fact, because we didn't get a chance to cancel today's order before they were delivered. Being closed for a few days is okay but any longer than that… Anyway, we were lucky, compared to the Hinkleys, and for that I'm very grateful. But none of the businesses downtown need a financial hit like this, not so close to the end of the year. And especially not that family, not after all they have been through. It's just…" Her voice trailed off and tears filled her eyes. "Too much. Far too much."

Mike wanted to reach out and take Julia's hand and comfort her. He could see the pain in her eyes, the regret. How he knew those feelings well. "No one knows why these kinds of things happen, Julia. All you can do is trust that there's a bigger purpose at work."

"And what purpose could that possibly be?"

His gaze went to the window. Two miles from this very spot, his wife's young life had ended in an instant. A bright, compassionate, kind and loving woman yanked from their lives. There was no reason or purpose behind that moment, not that Mike could see. "I don't know, Julia. I really don't know. But maybe, to be safe, you should go home and leave the cleaning until another day. He's already been here once. What's to stop him from coming back?"

"Daddy." Ginny tugged on Mike's sleeve. "Can I go draw?" She pointed at a table with a stack of paper and a box of markers and crayons.

"Sure." It would give him a chance to talk to Julia without little teapot ears listening.

Ginny slid off her stool, and hesitated, looking at the counter, then at the table. Julia sprung out of her seat. "You want me to carry your hot cocoa, Ginny?"

"Uh-huh. I can't cuz I gots a broken arm."

Julia chuckled. "I noticed."

And Mike had not. Again. He hadn't read the signs—the billboards for that matter—telling him that his daughter was struggling. If there was a category for dads who failed at parenting, he'd be at the top of the list.

"Here, Ginny, this will be easier than crayons." Julia gave Ginny a tablet with a fat stylus that was easier to hold in her nondominant hand. Ginny took it with a smile and set right to work on her first creation.

"Thank you," he said to Julia when she returned.

"No problem. And don't beat yourself up for not noticing. You've got a lot going on. Being distracted is part of the equation."

He scoffed. "I should be the one trying to make you feel better. You had a huge scare last night, your business is down, and here I am, darkening your doorstep again to humbly beg you to help me with my kid." A big part of him was relieved to see her in person. He knew that she was okay but seeing her face-to-face was evidence that nothing had happened to Julia. Thank goodness. "I don't think you should stay here alone anymore, even during the day. It's too dangerous."

Julia sighed. "Mike…"

"Hear me out, okay?" He fished the cabin keys out of his pocket and set them on the counter. "My friend is loaning me his brother's cabin for a few days. That friend happens to be Ginny's principal, who just had to give my daughter three days of an unofficial out-of-school suspension for getting into a fight on the playground. He advised me—strongly—to take a few days off and spend them with my daughter."

"I think that's a great idea."

"But as you can see, I'm not exactly father of the year. And frankly, the thought of three days with a daughter who barely gets along with me is…a little frightening because I'm still figuring out how to be the parent she needs. What if I make it worse?"

"You have all the parenting skills you need already. You're a veterinarian. You know how to take care of something that's hurting."

"If it has fur or feathers, yes, but when it comes to humans…" He sighed. "I am lost. I've never been someone who was especially good at interpersonal communications, especially with children."

"Well, first off, calling it interpersonal communications might be a mistake." She grinned.

His gaze went to his daughter, concentrating so hard on whatever she was drawing. He'd already called the office and told Jamie and Keesha to reschedule his appointments and then go home, promising to pay his employees for the days they would be out of work and throwing in a Christmas bonus as a thank-you to them for helping him keep the ship afloat. He was free, for all intents and purposes, to spend some quality time with his little girl. "I was hoping that I could convince you to come up to the cabin with us for a day. Maybe you and Ginny could have some one-on-one time. I think it would help her to adjust and deal with everything she has going on right now."

"I'm not a child psychiatrist, Mike. I'm just an occupational therapist. You should call someone else."

"There is no one else that Ginny trusts like you."

"I…" Her gaze went to Ginny, sitting at the table, still concentrating as she tapped on the screen and exchanged a digital brown crayon for a green one. "Like I said, I'm not a specialist in mental health. If I was…"

Her voice trailed off, and her entire body seemed to slump under some invisible weight. Emotions flickered in her features, and Mike knew, without a doubt, that she was thinking of the patient who had taken his own life earlier this year. She blamed herself, that was crystal clear, and was angry she had missed the signs that had been right in front of her.

He knew that guilt, even if his was in the form of a six-year-old who looked at him like he was letting her down every single day. "An older gentleman brought a terrier in to see me a couple years ago," Mike said. "Little thing, all mutt and heart."

Julia looked at him as if he'd grown a second head. "Okay."

Mike shifted his weight. Already, his attempt to build commiseration was failing. He just didn't have the words, at least not the right ones, to express sympathy and understanding. So he did what he always did—reverted to the impersonal chill of clinical terms. "It was just a routine checkup, you know, for shots and heartworm tests. But as I took a closer look at the dog, I knew something was wrong. When I palpated his belly, I found a mass so we did an X-ray right then and there. The terrier mix was diagnosed with an inoperable soft tissue sarcoma that had attached itself to the connective tissues around his spleen and liver. If those kinds of tumors are caught early, then surgery, radiation and chemo can save the dog and give him several years without a regrowth. But when it is a malignant high-grade sarcoma, the prognosis is much more grim."

"Okay…" she said again. "So what are you saying?"

"This owner waited far too long to bring his dog into the office. The sarcoma had invaded the terrier's lower body almost completely and was intertwined with too many major organs to make removal feasible. The dog died a week later. The owner was devastated and kept blaming himself for not bringing his pet in sooner."

"And this is supposed to help me feel better?"

"No…that's not my point." He let out a long breath. Why was this so hard? "What I meant is that—"

"That I'm not facing the truth that I missed the signs before it was too late?" She lowered her voice and leaned in closer. "I know the truth. I didn't notice the changes in Darryl and didn't call the right people in time to save him. His death is my fault, and there's nothing I can do to take that back."

"I'm not implying that, not at all. I'm just no good at this." He ran a hand through his hair and then tried again. "What I meant to say was that he blamed himself for something that wasn't his fault. He couldn't know what was happening right under that terrier's skin, and unless he was trained as a vet, he probably wouldn't have even noticed the mass because so much of it was deeply internal. Right up until the day he died, that little mutt was the happiest, most active dog you'd ever seen. He gave no outward sign that he was struggling or in pain. The owner did nothing wrong. Whatever mental issues Darryl was dealing with weren't your fault. The fact that he didn't share it or show any signs isn't your fault. And blaming yourself keeps you from moving on."

She turned away and got busy wiping the back counter, even though it was still sparkling clean. "You don't know anything about me."

A long pause, and then Mike said quietly, "I know what you're going through more than you think."

Before she could respond, the door to the shop opened, and a man in a thick blue coat emblazoned with an unfamiliar logo, along with the officer uniform of a white shirt and dark blue pants, walked in. The words *Arson Investigator* were inscribed across the left side of the jacket.

"Miss Beaumont?" the man said. "Or are you Mrs. Fitzgerald?"

"I'm Julia Beaumont," she replied. "My sister is not working today. How can I help you?"

"I'm Alan Cho, the head arson investigator for the state Division of Fire Prevention and Control. I have been called in to work with the local fire department and the ATF to investigate the string of fires in Crooked Valley, because the department doesn't have a full-time arson investigator." He showed her his credentials, waited for her to look at them and then tucked the badge away. "I'd like to ask you a few questions."

"Of course. Can I get you a cup of coffee?"

He gave her a grateful smile. "I'd sure appreciate a midday caffeine jolt. Whatever your strongest blend is, with a little sugar."

"Coming right up." She poured him a steaming mug of coffee and slid the cup, along with a container of sugar, across the counter.

As he poured the sugar into the cup, the officer glanced at Mike. "Uh…is there somewhere we can chat? I don't want to talk about this in front of your customers."

"This is Mike Byrne, Officer Cho. And he's a"— she glanced at Mike—"friend. And if it's okay, I'd like him to stay."

Well, *friend* wasn't a bad thing. But for some odd

reason, Mike felt disappointed with the label. Either way, Julia had asked him to stay for moral support, and that was the least he could do.

"Okay." Cho got out a notepad and a recorder and clicked his pen. He pressed Record, then dictated the time, location and Julia's name into the machine. "Miss Beaumont, where were you when the fire started last night?"

"I was with Mike. We were having dinner at his house, or about to, and, well…" She looked flustered, as if trying to explain the innocent evening had her confused. "And I got a text from my sister that the store next door was on fire."

"That would be Chloe Fitzgerald?"

"Yes. Normally we close at three, but she had come back to pick up a baby shower gift one of the customers gave her yesterday. That's when she noticed the fire starting and called the fire department."

Cho nodded, kept making notes, his gaze on the pad before him. "And what time was her text to you?"

Julia paused. "Close to six," Mike said. "I remember that because the delivery arrived just a few minutes before."

"That's right." Julia nodded. "It gets so dark so early in the winter here that it can be hard to keep track of time."

Cho just made a note. "And do you know Mrs. Fitzgerald's whereabouts before this call to 9-1-1?"

"If you're suggesting Chloe had anything to do with this, you haven't seen my sister." Julia laughed. "She's eight months pregnant and not exactly running around and sneaking down dark alleys. Plus, she's the last person to do anything like this, to our business or to the Hinkleys'."

"We suspect everyone until we know the truth, Miss Beaumont. I will be speaking to Mrs. Fitzgerald as well, of course." He turned to Mike. "Mr. Byrne, will you vouch for Miss Beaumont's statement?"

"Yes, of course," Mike said. "I was there when Chloe texted her. Julia told me about the text, then left to come here. I could hear the sirens for the fire trucks when Julia left my house."

The investigator asked a few more questions, but the information Julia had was limited. She'd arrived after the fire had already invaded the other building and hadn't seen anyone running from the scene or doing anything suspicious. She mentioned the stranger Chloe had seen and Cho said he would ask her sister about it later.

Cho seemed satisfied with her answers. The tension eased in his features, and he paused to drink his coffee. "Just to be safe, we're advising all the downtown buildings to close for a few days. It won't stop the arsonist from starting a fire, but it might prevent someone from getting hurt. The Crooked Valley Police Department is going to do extra patrols of this area every night. We will catch whoever is doing this, Miss Beaumont."

"It's a few days before Christmas, Officer Cho," Julia said. "The businesses here have already been hurt because customers are afraid to shop in a town where there have been so many fires. They need as much revenue as they can make before the end of the year."

"I realize that, Miss Beaumont, but my job is to keep the residents safe first and worry about bottom lines later." He flipped to a new page in his notebook. "Your business may have been the target for reasons we don't know yet. We found an incendiary device at the back of your building that matches the remains of the one at the store and matches what we have found at other fires." Frustration and exhaustion filled the lines in his face. It had been a long few months for the investigators, no doubt. "You were very lucky. The wind blew out the flame before it could catch on your building. Do you know of anyone who might have a personal vendetta against you or a reason to target your shop? Or do you have anyone in the military who frequents your establishment?"

She thought for a second, but Mike could have answered that question for her. Even after only knowing her for a short time, he was positive of one fact—no one who had ever met Julia Beaumont could dislike her. The chances of someone hating her enough to burn down her coffee shop were zero.

"There isn't anyone I can think of, Officer," she said. "I'm sorry."

Cho nodded and sipped his coffee. "I suspected as much. There hasn't seemed to be a lot of rhyme or reason to these fires. Several of them were connected to homes or businesses owned by people who work in the justice system—the county prosecutor, an attorney named Jim Daly and Judge William Bishop—but the others don't seem to have a connection to each other or to the justice department. Maybe this arsonist is just a firebug. Or maybe he has some other reasoning for who he is targeting. If you think of any connection, please let me know."

"I don't know the county prosecutor and I've met the other two but briefly," Julia said. "Either way, what would they have to do with me, my sister or this shop? Or the Hinkleys, for that matter?" Then she paused. "Wait a second. You said Jim Daly?"

Cho nodded.

"He was the defense attorney the Hinkleys used when their son, Darryl, was charged for the car accident he was in a year ago. I met Daly a couple times and testified as a character witness for Darryl because I was the occupational therapist they hired after his accident."

It was the same defense attorney Cal had mentioned in his conversation with Mike a few days ago. Like the officer had said, that connection probably didn't mean anything. Daly had worked with hundreds of criminals in his career. But it did make Mike worry that the police might be mistakenly targeting his friend.

Cho made a note. "Do you know where Darryl Hinkley is living now?"

"He died," Julia said softly. "Pretty soon after his case was dismissed. He just…wasn't the same after that accident."

"I'm sorry for your loss," Cho said. He crossed out Darryl's name on the pad. "We are looking into

Mr. Daly's past defendants. There could be some defendant who got sent to prison and had a vendetta against him and the rest of the justice system. But none of that links with the other fires this guy has set or with places like your coffee shop. We're asking everyone to keep their ears and eyes open. I can't force you to shut down, but I am making a very strong suggestion that you close up for a few days. We just don't want anyone to get hurt. We're looking at all possibilities, as I'm sure you know. If you can think of anyone who has experience with fire or who has a bone to pick with residents of this town, don't hesitate to call. Either of you." He handed her a slim white business card.

Julia nodded and tucked the card in her back pocket. The investigator finished his coffee, then said goodbye and headed out into the cold afternoon.

Mike thought of what Cal had told him about being a possible suspect because of his military training. He had no reason to think his friend would have anything to do with these fires, but it was clear the investigators didn't agree. Cho seemed like a man who understood reason, however, so hopefully the interview with Cal would go well. Mike made a mental note to reach out to his friend again this afternoon.

"Are you going to take the investigator's advice?" Mike asked Julia.

"I think I have to. I thought I was being all brave and strong being here to clean and get ready to reopen in a few days, but Officer Cho is right. It's too dangerous. I don't want to risk our employees' or Chloe's life in any way, and knowing her, she's stubborn enough to come back to work to help me. It's bad enough that she was here last night. If there hadn't been a wind and a hill…" Julia shook her head. "Besides, we don't have any customers anyway. Everyone I know is afraid to go out because Crooked Valley has become a very scary place to live. No one is safe anymore."

A chill ran up Mike's spine. To think of how close Julia had come to being a victim nearly undid him. She was right—no one was safe in this town while this lunatic was on the loose. It was a good thing he'd closed down the office for a few days. At least he'd know his employees would be safe at home, far from downtown.

Julia had come the closest of everyone he knew to being at the wrong end of the arsonist's match. A fierce need to protect her, to be sure she was far from danger, rose in his chest.

"Then come up to the cabin in the morning," he said, trying to keep the urgency, the worry, from his voice. "A day out in the woods might be just the stress reliever you need."

She worried her bottom lip. "Okay, but only for one day."

Thank goodness she'd said yes. At least for one day he'd know where she was and he wouldn't worry. All three of them would be safe, far from town and nestled deep in Mount Pine. But he didn't say any of that, didn't open his heart or expose the emotions that were rumbling in his chest. "I appreciate it, Julia. I really do."

His phone rang, and he flashed Julia an apologetic look. "It's the office. I need to get this."

"No problem. I'm going to go see how Ginny is doing," Julia said.

She crossed to the little girl, who was still completely immersed in the tablet. "How you doing, Ginny?"

Ginny smiled. "I made lots of pictures. I'm gonna show my daddy."

"You did. Good job." The moment with Mike had gotten intense there for a second. Julia could tell he was worried about her being at the coffee shop. But was his worry the normal worry of a friend or something more? And if it was something more, was she ready to deal with that?

No. Definitely not. So she redirected all her attention toward Mike's daughter instead. "This is great, Ginny. What picture did you draw first?"

"A snowman." She dotted two eyes in the center of the snowman's face. The drawing was crooked, the snowman more of a snowball, probably because Ginny had been working with her nondominant hand. The tablet had made it easier, but also a bit of a challenge. "I named him Winter."

"That's a great name for a snowman."

Ginny looked down at the screen. "I can't draw." She put her chin on her arm. "I'm a bad drawer."

Julia had seen this frustration and sadness in so

many of her patients. Learning how to do things in a new and different way was frustrating and tough. Lucky for Ginny, her cast would be off tomorrow. But until then, Julia could see a little girl with a well of emotions in her eyes. "Why don't I help you draw something?"

Ginny's face brightened. "You will?"

"Sure. Just tell me what you want to make a picture of. Let's try…" Julia pretended to think. In truth, she'd done this exercise with several children before who were struggling after a trauma. "A picture of you and someone else."

"Okay." Ginny struggled to use the stylus to make a small stick figure on one side of the screen. She sighed. "That doesn't look like me."

"What if you add your cast? Because that's part of you for right now."

"Yup, and it's pink cuz pink is my favorite color." She clicked on the fuchsia crayon and swiped it across the stick figure arm. Her face brightened with just that small touch.

"That's great. Does that look more like you now?"

Ginny was scribbling brown hair on top of the stick figure. "Uh-huh. It's got my hair. Daddy says my hair is difficult."

Julia bit back a laugh. She could imagine the vet struggling to tame those wild curls. Every time she'd seen Ginny, she'd noticed the little girl's hair needed some detangler and a lot of patience, two things she wasn't sure Mike had. "Now, let's draw someone beside you. Who's it going to be?"

Ginny stared at the blank space beside her self-portrait for a moment. "My mommy," she said softly. "I miss her a lot sometimes. But I don't always tell Daddy because it makes Daddy sad. He told me he's sad, too."

"I'm sure your daddy would love to see a picture of your mommy and that it wouldn't make him sad, because it would remind him how much you both loved her." And maybe that would open up a conversation between two people who were hurting. "I don't know what she looks like, so why don't you draw her?"

"She was really pretty," Ginny said. She started to make a circle with the stylus, then let out a long sigh when the lines didn't connect. "Can you draw the face?" She handed Julia the plastic tool. "My faces are all bad."

"They're not bad, Gin. They're just righties. And you and me are lefties, aren't we?" She did a light fist bump with her left hand and Ginny's left fingers. "Lefties are the best."

Ginny giggled. "Yup."

Julia created an oval on the page, then handed back the stylus. As tempted as she was to make it easier on Ginny by doing all the drawing, Julia knew the lesson was in the effort, not the results. "What color was your mommy's hair?"

"It was like mine but not so curly." Ginny selected a brown color and drew a series of straight lines down from the crown of the face. "She had really nice hair."

"I'm sure." Julia watched Ginny, letting the girl go at her own pace as she colored her mother's features. "Tell me more about your mommy. She sounds really nice."

"She liked apples and swimming and playing with me." Ginny's stylus swooped several more locks of hair in place. "Then she died."

The finality of those three words hit Julia hard. Such a horrible tragedy for a young child. No wonder she'd struggled so much at school. It had to be a scary, overwhelming life event. "I'm sure that made you really sad."

Ginny shrugged, but Julia could see tears threatening in the little girl's eyes. "Daddy says she went to Heaven. I wish I could go there."

"Me, too. My grandma is in Heaven, and I miss her a lot." Julia grabbed a blank sheet of paper and started drawing flowers with the crayons in a nearby box. That way, she was coloring with Ginny, not running an inquisition, which helped a child feel more at ease. With Darryl, Julia had drawn landscapes because nature was what seemed to calm Darryl down. Other kids had liked animals or beach scenes or simply rainbows. Whatever it was that would build a bridge for conversation, Julia would work it into their session. "My grandma really liked daisies. That's why I'm drawing some."

"My mommy liked dogs. Can I make a dog?"

"Sure. It's your picture." Julia started creating leaves but watched Ginny out of the corner of her eye. Ginny drew a brown blob that was probably a dog, then chose the red color and put a smile on the mommy face. "I like that picture, Ginny."

"T'ank you. I try really hard to be good," Ginny said as she went back to working on the blob dog. "And I know Daddy gets mad. But it's hard. I get mad cuz my mommy isn't here and doesn't read me stories anymore."

Poor kid. Such a big weight for her to shoulder. "You should tell your daddy that. I'm sure he'll understand."

Ginny shrugged. "I guess so."

Julia decided not to push the subject. Ginny was already looking pretty emotional, and Julia didn't want to make the girl clam up. "So, what else do you want to draw on your picture?" Julia started drawing an orange daisy.

"I gots to put on Mommy's eyes. But…" Ginny's face pinched, and tears welled in her eyes.

"It's okay, Ginny." Julia put a hand on Ginny's back. "Do you want me to draw the eyes for you?"

"You can't." A tear rolled slowly down her cheek. "You can't!" Then she slammed out of the chair and ran to one of the sofas. She curled into a ball and buried her face in the velvety fabric.

Mike was on his feet, heading for his daughter at the same time he hung up his call. "Ginny! What was that?"

Julia put up a hand to stop Mike from correcting the little girl. She met his gaze to tell him she had it under control. "It's all right, she didn't do anything wrong. She's just upset. Let's see where talking gets us first, okay?"

He nodded. Julia took a seat beside Ginny while Mike stood beside the couch, looking helpless and confused. "Ginny, you want to tell me why you got so mad?" Julia asked.

The little girl shook her head again and said a muffled "No."

"What happened?" Mike asked.

"We were drawing pictures. Ginny was drawing her mother, and we were talking. It was all going great but when she went to draw the rest of her mother's face, she burst into tears." Julia gestured toward the little girl, still crying into the sofa. Maybe Julia had pushed too hard or too far. The last thing she wanted to do was upset Ginny even more.

Mike didn't say anything for a long time. Then he knelt beside his daughter and began rubbing a circle on her back. "Hey, Gin. Can you talk to me?"

She shook her head.

"When you were drawing the picture of Mommy, did you get upset because…maybe you were having trouble remembering what she looked like?"

Ginny slowly peeled herself away from the couch and stared at her father, as if he'd suddenly discovered a secret. "Uh-huh."

Julia hadn't even thought of that. Her grandmother had died when she was much younger, and she'd never been through a loss that was as difficult as Mike and Ginny's.

"Gin, I forget sometimes, too," Mike said. "It's hard to remember everything about a person."

"You forget, too?"

He nodded. "Want me to show you a picture of her so you can remember?" He scrolled through his phone and brought up a shot of a stunning brunette with a wide smile.

Julia could immediately see that Mary Byrne had been a warm and loving person. She looked happy, strong, confident, and had undoubtedly been a fabulous mother and wife. Mike and Ginny had lost something special, and it was no wonder the two of them were having a hard time getting over that.

"Mommy!" Ginny said, taking the phone and holding it in both hands. "She's so pretty."

"She is. And so are you, because you look a lot like her," Mike said. "It doesn't matter if you remember what color eyes she had, Ginny. Because all the best parts of Mommy didn't go anywhere." Mike tapped the space above Ginny's heart. "She's right here inside of you."

"She is?"

Mike's features softened, almost radiating with the deep love he had for his daughter. In that moment, the uptight veterinarian who used too many big words disappeared, and he became an ordinary father having a difficult conversation with his child. "You have her smile and her eyes, and you are just as smart and curious as she was. She would be so proud of you."

"T'ank you, Daddy." Ginny reached out and hugged her father for a brief, tight second, then she climbed off the couch. "I'm gonna finish my picture!"

"Do you want my phone?" Mike asked her. "So you have the picture?"

"Nope. I know Mommy right here." She tapped her chest and beamed. A few seconds later, she was hunched over the tablet again.

"Wow. That was amazing," Mike said. "You brought so much out of her just from a simple drawing."

"I didn't do anything. You did all the hard work."

He scoffed. "There's a reason all these kids"—he waved at the clothesline of drawings hanging in the coffee shop—"have come to you to heal. You don't just help them learn how to do daily life. You help them learn to open up, too."

"Not all of them," she said softly.

"You don't give yourself enough credit, Julia. There's just something about you. You..." His voice trailed off, and it seemed as if he was about to say something, but he shook his head. "You're good at your job."

They wandered back to the counter. She topped off both of their coffees and took a seat beside him at the granite bar. "Like I said, it wasn't me. You spoke from the heart and said exactly what Ginny needed to hear."

He sighed. "That's the problem. I don't do that. I didn't do it with my wife, either. I told her I loved her a handful of times, not nearly often enough. I'm just not the kind of guy who opens his heart."

"I'd disagree because you just did it. I was there. Maybe it's harder for you to tell other people how you feel, but you were open with Ginny, and that helped her know that she isn't alone in what she's going through. That's huge, Mike." Julia sipped her coffee and watched Ginny finish one picture, then start another. "Maybe a few days away with just you and Ginny and no distractions of work or school will help her open up more and get some of these emotions out that are causing her to act up in school. What time are you heading to the cabin?"

"I thought we'd head up first thing in the morning, after Ginny's doctor's appointment. They're taking her cast off tomorrow, thank goodness. We should be done there by ten and be on the road right after. I'm going to try to beat the storm that's rolling in tomorrow night."

"Why don't I get there around the same time you do? That way I can help Ginny unpack and work on teaching her how to start strengthening her wrist again, and talk to her as well." She put the officer's mug into the sink, then washed and dried it.

Already he was looking forward to seeing her again tomorrow. He liked Julia more and more every time he saw her. "That works for me. I'll text you when we're on the road." He gestured toward the empty coffee shop. "Want me to help you close up? Walk you to your car?"

She hesitated, then glanced out the window at the charred skeleton next door. "I would like that. Even in broad daylight it's hard to feel…"

"Safe," Mike finished. He couldn't agree more.

# Chapter Seven

Without the coffee shop to go to, and no patients to see, Thursday morning loomed like a shadow over Julia. She checked her bank account and reminded herself for the thousandth time that she couldn't avoid working indefinitely. The coffee shop provided some income, but it wasn't nearly as much as her OT work had paid. If she went back part-time, working with maybe one or two patients, it would be enough to close the financial gap.

Even the thought of going back to work, however, filled her with a sense of dread. What if she got it wrong again? What if she said the wrong thing or didn't notice the signs or missed a crucial trigger for one of her charges? Maybe she should be the one in therapy, not just her patients, because she clearly hadn't gotten over what happened with Darryl.

*Blaming yourself keeps you from moving on.* Mike's words came back to her, haunting the edges of her thoughts, demanding she see things in a different way. It also reminded her that she was great at giving advice to other people that she didn't take herself.

Either way, she had a month or so before she really needed to start worrying about making money. Maybe by then the arsonist would be caught, Crooked Valley would go back to its usual sleepy small-town state and the coffee shop would pick up again. And life would return to normal.

Or whatever normal looked like. Julia wasn't sure she knew anymore.

For this afternoon, there was the cabin on the mountain, Mike and his daughter. The sooner Julia got there, the sooner the day could be done, and she could stop thinking about how the two-person Byrne family had begun to invade her heart. Ginny's drawing had caused Julia to imagine, for just a second, her and Mike and his adorable little girl all together at Christmas. Forming a family. A future.

She'd shut down those thoughts almost as quickly as they appeared. She couldn't get close to anyone like that again—couldn't put anyone at risk and couldn't bear to have her heart broken one more time. Get in, get out and get home. That would be her motto for today.

The forecast called for temps in the low thirties, dropping into the teens at night. Julia would be home well before the storm moved in, but she dressed in layers anyway. If there was one thing she'd learned about living in Colorado, it was flexibility with the weather. A morning blizzard could be melted by afternoon, or a sunny day could turn blustery at a moment's notice.

She debated wearing boots, but in the end opted for tennis shoes, stowing her boots in the trunk of her car. If it started to snow, she'd have plenty of time to switch. When Mike texted her a little after ten, she pulled on a dark navy parka, checked that she had gloves and a hat in the pocket then started heading toward the cabin.

Out of the corner of her eye, she spotted a red pickup truck behind her as she got on Golden Byway and took the long, desolate road out of town. Not an entirely uncommon thing to see in a mountainous state like Colorado, but the truck looked familiar. She didn't know anyone who drove a truck like that, at least not that she could remember, and dismissed the thoughts as she turned right onto the road that led to Mount Pine. The pickup was in her rearview for a second longer, before he pulled off a side road and disappeared.

She was getting skittish, that was all, after the fires and the one that came so close to Three Sisters Grindhouse. People she knew had been hurt—thankfully not physically, but financially, mentally, emotionally—and it had the whole town on edge. The arsonist had quickly become the only topic of conversation in Crooked Valley. Where would he strike next? Who was at risk? And why couldn't law enforcement catch him?

And most of all—did he have something personal against Julia or Chloe? Why would he target the coffee shop otherwise? Why did he hurt anyone at all? Was it personal or just some kind of sick game?

Julia made one more turn, onto the long, hilly, curvy road that led up the mountain and into the woods. The light narrowed with every foot as she drove deeper and deeper into a thick forest. Even in the middle of winter, the tall, bare trees and thick, full pines stood like sentries huddled together, guarding their own. Two miles up the winding mountain road she saw a row of cabins, none of them looking occupied, before she reached the one where Mike's SUV was parked in the driveway.

A light blanket of snow from the previous storm carpeted the entire area. Up here in the mountains, the flurries had already started, but they were still light, and the weatherman had said the real storm wouldn't start until after five. It was at least ten degrees colder on the mountain than in the valley. Leaving her boots in the trunk, Julia grabbed her tote bag and climbed the porch stairs.

The door opened before she could knock, and Ginny stood there, all smiles and uncombed hair. "Miss Julia! I got my cast off! Look at my arm! It's all better!" She raised her arm. The skin where the cast had been was pale, but in no time at all, Ginny would be back to normal.

"That's awesome, Ginny. I can't wait for you to show me what you can do now."

"My daddy says we are gonna stay here and play in the snow." Ginny kept talking as Julia came inside, brushed the snow off her shoes then hung her coat on the hook by the door. Heat radiated from the woodstove in the center of the cabin, a welcome environment after even a few minutes outside in the mountain winter. "I wanna make snow angels and bake cookies and look for Santa."

"That's a lot for three days," Mike said as he emerged from the kitchen, his voice sounding exhausted already. "Especially for a father who doesn't know how to bake."

"But it's almost Christmas, Daddy. We have to make cookies. Santa needs them." She dashed off to the dining room, then came back. "Daddy, look at my picture. I drew a picture of a Christmas tree, cuz now I can use my leftie hand and I can make good drawings. This one has you and me and Miss Julia and a kitty cat."

Mike arched a brow. "Miss Julia and a kitty cat?"

Ginny nodded. "Uh-huh."

"We don't have a kitty cat, Ginny. And Miss Julia lives in her own house."

"I know that." Ginny toed a circle on the hardwood floor. "But I asked Santa for a kitty cat, and I've been a good girl." She paused a second. "Well... I tried to be a good girl."

Mike and Julia exchanged a look of mirth, neither of them reminding Ginny that she'd just been sent home from school for a few days for fighting. "It's a nice drawing, Ginny," her father said. "We should hang it on the fridge."

That wasn't the answer she wanted, clearly, because she hung her head and trudged back to the table. Mike sighed.

"Seems like a vet wouldn't have a hard time getting a kitten," Julia whispered to him.

"You're right. I see lots of animals who need a home in my practice," he said. "It's been a long time since we've had a pet. Our family dog passed away a few months before my wife died, and it just seemed so…overwhelming to add one more thing into the mix after Mary was gone."

"Maybe it's time for a step outside that comfort zone, Mike." She shrugged and gave him a smile because she knew Chloe would say the exact same thing to Julia—and had, several times. At least once a week, Chloe told Julia she should go back to work as an occupational therapist, and at least once a week, Julia said no. She told Chloe it was a fear of hurting someone else by missing the signs of depression, but deep down inside, Julia knew it was more. She was scared to fail, scared that she was bad at her job and scared of getting close to someone else. So she put up walls and refused all attempts at getting back into the field she loved. "Ignore all that. The pot is calling the kettle black, because I'm doing the same thing as you, avoiding the things that scare me."

He chuckled. "Probably not a good idea for us to both do that, because then we're avoiding everything together."

"Good friends encourage each other to get out of their comfort zones," she said. The word *friends* inserted some emotional distance and allowed Julia to tell herself that all she wanted with the handsome veterinarian was friendship. Maybe if she said it often enough, she'd believe it, too. "Which means you should get a kitty cat."

"Maybe." Mike glanced at his daughter, who had started working on another picture at the table. "Let me get through Christmas first."

She could only imagine how difficult the holiday was for him as a single parent and a widower, especially because Mike had to have hundreds of memories of holidays past with his late wife. Maybe there was a way for Julia to make some of that easier for both Mike and Ginny. That wasn't getting emotionally involved—it was just helping. Right? "By the way, baking cookies is really good occupational therapy for Ginny, and a distraction from all the other stuff going on for her and in town. I'd be glad to help with that if you have the ingredients."

"Kitchen is pretty well stocked, and I brought eggs and milk up here with me, so if you're volunteering to stir whatever you need to mix together, have at it. You've seen my grocery cart. You know my level of cooking skills."

Julia laughed. "You're never too old to learn a new skill, Dr. Byrne."

"While you're at it, maybe you can teach Ginny how to do braids and ponytails." They crossed to the dining room. Mike waved at Ginny's head while she went on drawing. Her curly hair stuck out in all directions with little tangles along the back and sides. There had been a clear attempt at combing on one side that hadn't gotten very far. "We had a crisis this morning."

"I can see that." Poor Mike. He was so out of his depth when it came to girlie things. She should help him out—as a friend, not as someone who was falling for the vet and his lovable little girl. Julia bent down. "Ginny, why don't you go get me your hairbrush and comb, and I'll help you put in some braids before we get started on baking cookies?"

"But I don't know how to do braids," Ginny said.

"Well, you're never too old to learn a new skill, Gin." Mike winked. "The brush and comb are on the bathroom counter."

Ginny took off down the hall, a happy ball of energy that Julia couldn't help but adore. She sighed. There was no way Julia was going to get out of this day without getting more attached to Ginny—and her handsome father.

"Thank you," Mike said. "I know I keep saying this, but I truly appreciate your help more than you know."

"Oh, I'm not doing all the work, Mike," Julia said to him, an idea forming in her head as she spoke. She headed into the kitchen, found an empty spray bottle and filled it with water. "I'm teaching. You're coming along for the lesson, too."

"Me? I'm all thumbs when it comes to girl hair," he said. "All I cause are meltdowns and more tangles."

She laughed. "If you can do surgery on a cat, I assure you that you can put in a braid."

Ginny skidded into the foyer with the comb and brush in one hand and a pile of brightly colored hair ties in the other. "I'm ready, Miss Julia!"

"Okay, let's head to the kitchen table, since there's more light in that room." Julia pulled a small mirror out of her bag—something she used with clients who needed to relearn ordinary tasks like putting on makeup or fixing their hair, like Ginny was doing—and set it in front of one of the chairs. Ginny scrambled into the seat and slapped the brush onto the table, nearly knocking the brush to the floor in her eagerness. "My goodness, you're a wiggly worm today, aren't you?"

Ginny giggled and shook her body even more. "I'm a wiggly worm!"

"Well, let's get those wiggles out now so you're not all squirmy when we're making your hair pretty. Here, I'll get my wiggles out, too." Julia undulated her arms and hips and shook her body, which only made Ginny giggle more and echo the movements. "Whoo! I feel much better now. How about you?"

Ginny nodded and did her best to sit still. "Yup! I'm better, too!"

Mike stared at Julia as if she had just parted the Red Sea. "How did you do that?"

Julia sifted through the pile of hair ties and found two matching pink elastics. "Do what?"

"Flip that switch that goes from wild to well-behaved in a certain small human?" He nodded toward his daughter, who was now being calm and patient.

Julia supposed she should feel embarrassed for being so silly, but she wasn't. The best way to connect with a child, Julia had found, was to talk to them in their language, on their level. Going all "adult" just created distance and made the therapy she was doing seem clinical and cold, which only resulted in the child being less cooperative. If she turned their therapy sessions into more of a game, kids willingly and enthusiastically participated. "It's easy," Julia said as she placed the comb in Mike's hands. "You just have to think like a kid."

"I barely think like an adult never mind a kid," Mike grumbled. "I speak animal, remember?"

"Well, Dr. Doolittle, try the techniques you use to calm a feral cat or a rowdy dog. You have all the skills and instincts you need already."

"Labradors don't have to have their hair braided, though." He raised a doubtful brow as he shifted into place behind Ginny's wild riot of curls. "Okay, where do I start?"

"Wait. I don't think you're ready yet," Julia said. "Did you get your wiggles out yet?"

Ginny spun around. "Yeah, Daddy. You can't have the wiggles cuz it'll hurt my head. You gotta get 'em all out. Like this." She stood in the chair and waved her arms and shook her head.

Julia could see the hesitation in the by-the-book veterinarian's face. For a second, she thought he would refuse, and then...

Mike began to wiggle, just a little, starting with

moving his shoulders an imperceptible amount. "Like this?"

Ginny giggled. "No, Daddy, like this." Her arms undulated up and down, and she moved her head from side to side.

"Hmm," Mike said. "Maybe like this?" He shivered his hips.

"Daddy, you gotta move your *whole* body. Like me." Ginny wiggled up and down, back and forth, shaking her hips and waving her arms. "See?"

"Let me try it." Mike shifted his hips side to side, slow at first, then faster, pumping his arms up and down, lifting and dropping his shoulders. He even shook out one leg, then the other. Then he wobbled his face and head. Ginny giggled and Julia laughed so hard she clutched her belly.

"Yay, Daddy! No more wiggles. I'm so proud of you!" Ginny leaned over and fell against Mike's chest. He wrapped his arms around her and gave her a tight hug before settling her back in the chair.

"Proud of you, too, Ginster," he said softly.

"Oh my," Julia gasped as she tried to catch her breath in the middle of a laugh. "That was the funniest thing I've ever seen."

"I can be funny."

"True. I have heard you joke before. But this"—she wiggled her hips and arms—"took your comedic skills to a new level."

"Like you said, Julia, I always had those skills. I just needed a reminder of why I should use them."

He pressed a kiss to the top of Ginny's head. She beamed up at him.

A rush of emotion ran through Julia. To see the two of them find their way back to being a family filled her heart with gratitude and love.

Wait…love? No, not that word. Maybe strong affection. Caring. Connection. Either way, she was touched to have been part of this moment. She had that same mixture of pride and fulfillment that she used to have with her clients when they were able to make big strides in their recovery. For the first time since Darryl's death, Julia missed the work she had once loved: the process of helping a child get back to being a child again.

Maybe there was a way she could return to that career, starting with Ginny. And after Christmas, she should call the physician group she had worked with and explore the possibility of going back, one patient at a time. Maybe.

"Well, now that no one has the wiggles, we have a headful of tangles to brush out." Julia spritzed Ginny's hair with water to make it easier to work with, then picked up the wide-toothed comb. "Work out the tangles a little at a time. But gently." Julia demonstrated the technique for Mike by catching a hunk of Ginny's hair, holding tight to the top and taking her time to comb out the tangles, all without pulling on Ginny's scalp.

"Got it." Mike took the comb and repeated what Julia had done, going slow and showing the same precision and care he undoubtedly had in his practice with animals. Ginny complained a few times, but Mike adapted his technique as he went along, and a few minutes later, her hair was tangle-free.

"Now we're going to do two braids." She picked up the comb and switched places with Mike. He stood close to her, close enough that she caught the spicy scent of his cologne. It distracted her and made her wonder if *friends* was really the right word to define their relationship. "Um…you draw a line like this." Her hand shook a little as she pulled the comb along Ginny's part. Then she handed Mike one of the pink elastics. "We'll do this together, one of us on each side. And, Ginny?"

The little girl glanced up. "Uh-huh."

"Your job is to watch what we do in the mirror. One day, you'll be a big girl and you can do this all by yourself." Julia gathered her half of Ginny's hair and watched Mike do the same. She talked him through dividing the hair into three plaits, then alternating one over the other until he reached the end. After they secured the braids with elastics, she came over to his side and checked his work. Mostly neat and precise and even. "Not bad for an amateur."

He grinned. "I have to admit, that wasn't as complicated as it looks."

"Daddy, you did a good job!" Ginny said, turning her head from side to side as she looked at her reflection. "Almost as good as Miss Julia."

Mike chuckled. "Thanks for the honest review, Gin. I'll be sure to add it to my Yelp page."

"Would you look at that? Another joke from Dr.

Byrne. You're becoming a veritable stand-up comedian." Then she met his dark brown eyes and gave
him a smile. She liked this man more and more all
the time. "You surprise me sometimes."

"Is that a good thing?" he asked.

"I think so." She couldn't speak of the tangle of
emotions inside her heart right now, or how it would
take a lot more than a comb and some patience to
undo the mess she was feeling.

"Daddy!" Ginny had scrambled out of the chair
and was now tugging on Mike's sleeve. "Can we
decorate? I wanna decorate."

"Decorate?" Mike said. "I thought you wanted to
bake cookies."

Ginny flipped out her fingers and counted out a
list. "I wanna decorate and then I wanna bake cookies and then I wanna make snow angels. Cuz it's
almost Christmas and we gotta have cookies and
snow angels."

"We can't decorate this house because we…"
Mike paused and thought a minute. "Wait. Maybe
we can. Give me a second." He grabbed his coat from
the hook by the door, then hurried outside.

Julia looked at Ginny, and the two of them shrugged.
It was only a second later before Mike was coming
back inside, carrying a heavy box. "I forgot I picked up
some of the Christmas decorations the other day. I store
the outdoor decorations at the office because there's
more room there than in my little one-car garage." He
opened the lid of the box and peered inside. "Looks

like we have what we need to hang up the outside lights and maybe set up the nativity scene by the fireplace."

"Yay!" Ginny jumped up and down. "Can I help, Daddy? I wanna do the lights and I wanna put the baby Jesus in his crib."

Julia thought how nice—and normal—this moment was. It was as if the fires and danger existed on another planet far from here. That was a blessing for all three of them, to be sure.

"Ginny, you can help with the lights if you get your coat and boots—" Before he even finished the sentence, Ginny was off like a rocket. Mike chuckled. "If I'd known it was that easy to keep her happy, I'd have been hanging lights all year."

"She's a great kid." Julia watched the six-year-old bundle of energy wrestle into her coat. "I know you think you're failing her in some way, Mike, but she adores you, and I think you're doing great."

"Thank you, Julia. I guess I needed to hear that more than I realized." He picked up one of the elastics they hadn't used and turned it over in his hand. "It's been the simple things that have been the hardest for me to deal with, like braids and bath time. And this is going to sound silly but..."

"But what?" she asked when he didn't continue.

"Successfully braiding Ginny's hair today made me feel so much more confident. Like maybe I can handle this single-parent thing."

"You are totally handling this single-parent thing, Mike. I admire how hard you work with Ginny and what a great dad you are." And there her heart went, getting all warm and fuzzy again. So far, her track record for not getting closer to the handsome veterinarian and his winsome daughter today was in the negative numbers.

"Miss Julia!" Ginny was sitting on the floor, trying to jam her feet into her boots. "You gots to help, too! Do you got a coat?"

"I have a coat and gloves, but my boots are in the car. Here, let me help you with these, and then I'll go get mine." Julia bent down and switched the left boot Ginny was unsuccessfully trying to jerk onto her right foot for the correct boot. Julia slid the rubber boots over Ginny's thick socks, lessening some of the work the little girl's newly healed wrist had to do.

The three of them got their winter clothes on and headed out to the porch. Ginny brought her teddy bear and sat him against one of the railings so he could watch them hang lights. While Mike untangled the strings of lights and Ginny raced back and forth on the porch telling her bear all about Christmas, Julia walked down to her car to switch out her tennies for boots. Just as she opened the trunk, a flash of something silver in the woods caught her eye. She straightened and scanned the area. There was always the chance of a late-hibernating bear looking for one more snack before he took his winter nap. Except bears weren't silver, and what she'd seen hadn't had fur.

Nothing moved. It was probably her imagination. Julia brushed it off. She pulled on her boots, stowed her tennies by the front door and then joined Mike and Ginny on the porch. The three of them began draping multicolored lights across the porch railings, just using plastic ties that Mike also had in his trunk so they could easily take the lights down again before they left. Giant egg-shaped bulbs in red, green, yellow and blue added a splash of color to the brown of the cabin and the thick snow that had begun falling. The thick white flakes added a hush to the air, carpeting the woods with a blanket of silence.

Just as Ginny started singing an off-key, and slightly incorrect, version of "Santa Claus Is Coming to Town," Julia swore she heard the crack of a branch. Ginny kept singing, and Julia brushed off the sound. Heavy snow was bound to break a branch or two.

"You better watch out," Ginny sang, "you better not cry, you better be good because I know why…"

Julia grinned and joined in with her, not bothering to correct the mistaken lyrics. "Santa Claus is coming to town."

"He sees you when you're sleeping," Mike piped in with a rich baritone. There was a quick pause as both Ginny and Julia stared at Mike like he was a stranger. "What? I can sing. I just usually choose not to."

"Daddy's singing, too!" Ginny's joy sparkled in her eyes. "Let's all sing!"

Julia and Mike exchanged a glance, then they both nodded. In near-perfect harmony, the three of them belted out the chorus while Mike wove the lights in and out of the railing, Julia wrapped the post and

Ginny danced between them with her bear as her dance partner.

When they finished, laughter filled the crisp air. "I forgot how much fun all this can be," Julia said. It had been a couple years since she had decorated her apartment for Christmas or been home with all three of her sisters to put up a tree. Julia usually spent the day with Chloe and Bob, whose house was always a Christmas explosion, because it was Chloe's favorite holiday. Julia had missed these simple moments of stringing lights and singing carols. Of being part of a family that, for this moment, in this remote location, felt a lot like her own.

"Me, too," Mike said. "I'm glad you two reminded me."

"Let's sing another one, Daddy! Let's sing 'Rudolph'!"

And so they did, creating an impromptu Christmas carol concert on the porch as they hung up the last string of lights. When they were done, Mike flipped the switch to *on*, and the three of them stood in the yard, marveling at the cheery sparkling bulbs, a bright beacon on a snowy day.

"Beautiful," Mike said. But he wasn't looking at the lights. He was looking directly at Julia.

Her face heated. Did he mean she was beautiful? Was the handsome vet attracted to her? If so, how did that change the equation?

It didn't, Julia told herself. She was only going to be in their lives for this one afternoon and then walk away. Protect her heart, protect them from disappointment and hurt. At least, that's what she told herself as they headed for the front door and she changed the subject. "That storm seems to be arriving early," Julia said. "It's starting to come down hard."

"You should probably hit the road pretty soon, then," Mike said as he started to help Ginny out of her snow-covered coat. He shook out Ginny's hat and hung it on a hook. "I'd check the forecast, but I can't get a signal on my cell this far up the mountain. Either way, it's probably best to leave before dark because it's dangerous to go down those mountain roads when they're slippery and icy."

Julia glanced at the sky. Every minute, it looked a little darker, more foreboding. She hadn't noticed the storm getting so much stronger when they were having fun hanging the lights, but now she could see how thick the snow had become. Two or three inches had already fallen, and would undoubtedly be followed by more. But Julia didn't want to leave. Not just yet. She slipped out of her clunky, heavy boots and put on her dry tennis shoes. "I should be fine for a little bit. At least long enough to help you set up the nativity."

Ginny crossed her arms over her chest and pouted. "But you said you'd bake cookies with me."

Julia bent down to Ginny's level. She hated to disappoint the little girl. Whipping up some cookie dough and throwing a batch in the oven shouldn't take that long. She'd leave as soon as the first batch was baking. Mike could handle it from there. "I did promise that, didn't I?" She raised her gaze to Mike's. "I can stay and do that, too. If it's okay with your dad."

"I would like that very much, Julia, but"—he glanced out the window again—"if the weather gets worse, you have to promise me you'll put your safety first. We can go in my SUV."

"You don't have to do all that, Mike. I can drive."

"Let me take care of you, Julia. Don't be as stubborn as me." He started to smile, and then his face froze. A chill filled the space in the foyer. "Oh no," Mike whispered. "Not here, too."

A heavy stone of foreboding dropped in her stomach as Julia slowly rose and pivoted to look at whatever Mike had just seen. She knew what was happening before she saw it, and even though she whispered a quick prayer that they were mistaken, she *knew*.

A fire was beginning to curl up the side of the cabin next door. It was maybe thirty yards away, separated by a dozen trees—and a pile of chopped wood that stretched between the cabins like one long dynamite fuse. There had been a tarp protecting the wood earlier, but it was gone now, leaving the logs exposed. All it would take was a gust of wind and the flames would rush along that fence of firewood and hit this house.

How could this have happened? There'd been no lightning. No one was staying in the other cabins. There was no reason a fire could spontaneously begin next door. There was only one answer—

The evil that had been setting Crooked Valley on fire had followed them here. Why?

"Daddy! There's a fire!" Ginny pointed at the orange flames eagerly running up the wooden siding of the cabin next door, inches away from the wood pile, and any hope that Julia had that her eyes were deceiving her disappeared. The house next door was on fire, and their lives were suddenly in very real danger.

"We need to get out of here. Now." Mike grabbed Ginny's coat and started helping her arms into the sleeves. Julia bent down beside him and fastened the zipper, then grabbed Ginny's hat and tugged it on her head as Mike pulled back on his boots. Julia grabbed her coat just in time to see the flames leap to the pile of dried wood and race across the top like a hungry animal.

Heading straight for their cabin.

"Get in my car!" Mike shouted.

They ran for the SUV, shoving on hats and mittens as they hurried across the yard. Julia stopped short just as Mike opened the passenger's side door. "Mike, look." The two front tires had been slashed and were beginning to go flat. Julia spun to the right and saw the same thing had been done to her car. They couldn't drive, not in these wintry conditions, and not on flat tires. "Someone doesn't want us leaving," she said under her breath, and fear curled a tight fist inside her chest.

Mike quickly scanned the area. "He's out there. Somewhere."

Oh no. Why would the arsonist follow them? Why would he target Mike and Ginny? Or Julia, for that matter? He had to have known there were people in the cabin, because it was the only cabin with cars and lights on—and the three of them had been standing outside mere minutes ago. And yet, he'd chosen to set the cabin on fire anyway.

A chill snaked up her spine as she realized that he must have *watched* them stringing lights, singing carols. He'd watched them—and still decided to take the lives of two adults and a small child. What kind of evil person did that?

Behind them the flames had reached the cabin where all three of them had been a moment ago. The wind fed the fire, amping it up with each gust, making it too strong to be doused by the falling snow. The scent of gasoline was pungent and strong. And far too close.

"Come on. We have to go on foot." Mike took Julia's hand in one hand, then scooped up Ginny on the other side. They started to run, but after two steps, Julia realized her mistake.

"My boots! I left them in the house.". The snow was already soaking into her tennis shoes, replacing her socks with cold puddles. She wouldn't last long in a winter storm without boots.

"It's too late, Julia." He tugged her forward, toward the pine trees, the cover of brush.

Even as he said the words, she could see the fire overtaking the small cabin, eagerly devouring the

Christmas lights they had just hung. The sweet moment the three of them had was being erased.

It was a two-mile trip down the mountain, just to get to the byway. Another two miles back to town. On foot, they'd never make it before dark. How were they going to get back to safety?

The three of them ducked behind a blue spruce that towered over them, at least fifty feet into the sky. The snow had weighed down the branches until they almost brushed against the ground. The thick tree limbs provided some cover, but not enough. With Ginny in a bright pink coat, they were easy to spot.

Mike held Ginny to his chest. Her eyes were wide, and the normally chatty six-year-old was silent. He fished in his back pocket, found his phone and swiped up to see the screen. "Do you have a signal?"

Julia raised her phone as high as she could. She turned left, then right. "Nothing." Oh no. How were they going to get out of here? There was no way to get help, no way to tell anyone what was happening.

Mike's gaze met Julia's, strong, serious. "We have to get lower to get service. We can't stay here, Julia, and we can't go back. We have no choice but to go down."

The snow was falling faster now, multiplying over and over again. It deadened the sound in the woods but also provided a big fat arrow showing the arsonist where they had gone, if the bright pink coat wasn't enough of a beacon for him.

They had no car, no snowmobiles and no easy way to reach the bottom of Mount Pine. The arsonist had to have used some kind of vehicle to get up here. Maybe he'd been dumb enough to leave the keys in the ignition and they could take that. But even Julia knew that was a foolish hope. "Oh, Mike, how are we going to get out of here?"

"We stick together." Mike hoisted Ginny higher on his left hip. "Let's go."

Ginny clung to Mike's neck and buried her face in his chest. "I'm scared, Daddy."

"I've got you, baby girl. I've got you." He hugged her tight, then started moving. Julia kept up beside him, the two of them picking their way toward the road. Wherever she could, Julia tried to step on a bare patch of ground because of a tree blocking the snowfall, but those spots were few and far between. Already her feet were cold and wet. Another few feet and they would be on the road, where they should be able to move much faster, she told herself, and get to someplace where she could warm up. There was no reason to think the arsonist would follow them, right?

But even as she thought that, a red pickup emerged from behind another cabin and began crawling down the road. The same red pickup she'd seen in her rearview mirror this morning. The same red pickup that had been parked in the lot across from Daisy Blue and the Grindhouse on the night of the fire.

She tugged on Mike's sleeve. He turned to look over his shoulder and through the trees that edged the snowy road. "Why is he following us?" Mike whispered.

Julia could only shake her head because she was

too scared of the answer. If the arsonist was following her on purpose, then he wasn't here to burn the cabin down—he was here to hurt Julia and by extension, Mike and Ginny. The pickup revved its engine and turned toward the bank where Mike, Ginny and Julia were. Mike grabbed Julia's hand again and they spun around, breaking for the trees and ducking into the forest. Immediately, her feet were plunged into deep, cold snow. But they kept running, Ginny holding tight to her father's neck, disappearing deeper and deeper into the woods.

It seemed like they had run forever before they stopped behind another towering spruce. They could no longer see the road or any of the cabins. A dark curl of smoke rose toward the sky, stark and deathly against the white of the storm. To think they could have still been in the cabin…

No. She wouldn't go there. Instead, she'd just be grateful to God for getting them out of there before anything could happen. Somehow, He would get them out of the woods and back to Crooked Valley safely, too.

"I think he's gone," Mike said. "Maybe we're far enough down to get a signal. Check your phone."

She did as he asked. "Still nothing." Disappointment turned into fear in Julia's gut, but she tried to keep the feelings at bay. They were together, and even though they were cold and a little lost, they were safe for now. *Focus on things you are grateful for, not problems you can't solve.*

Mike held up his cell, too. "Same here. Not a

single bar." His attention dropped to her feet and concern filled his features. "Oh, Julia, you must be freezing. Your shoes are soaked all the way through."

"I'm fine." But that was a lie. She could feel the cold seeping into her bones. A deep ache was already traveling up her ankles. She thought of everything she had learned in school about what kind of damage frostbite could do to someone's extremities and how quickly she could lose her toes. No, she refused to focus on that. They would get to safety and get warm before that happened. They had to.

"It's getting colder," Mike said, as if he'd read her mind. "And the wind is picking up. It's going to feel like it's below zero once the sun goes down. And with this snow…"

"I know." Neither of them needed to say anything about how little time she would have once it got that cold. In less than a half hour, permanent damage could set in, and she could end up losing her toes. They had to get out of here and get back to town before it was too late.

The sound of a breaking branch came from just behind them. So close, it sounded like the crack of a rifle. Julia glanced over her shoulder.

And there he was. The arsonist was short and muscular in a way that seemed like he could break a person in two. His face was partially hidden by the hood of his parka and a buff he had pulled over the lower half of his face. She could see the edges of a beard where the buff had slipped a little. But it was his eyes that terrified Julia. Dark, menacing and full of rage.

Something familiar nagged at Julia but whatever it was disappeared in a cloud of fear because the arsonist raised the gun in his hand, and all Julia could do was scream. "Run!"

Mike made the same split-second decision. He grabbed Ginny with both arms and dashed into the woods, with Julia right beside him. A bullet whizzed past Mike's head, and they began to run even faster, weaving between the trees, leaving a clear trail behind them in the snow. A trail they could hear the arsonist starting to follow.

## Chapter Eight

Time.

They needed enough time and distance to cover their tracks so they could all take a moment to catch their breath and hopefully get warm. They'd been slogging through the snow for at least twenty minutes. The thick, wet blanket of precipitation was only getting thicker and heavier as the storm strengthened, and Mike was starting to seriously worry about Julia and Ginny. His daughter was bundled in her winter coat and tight against his body, but she was too little to be out in this weather for long. And Julia… Those tennis shoes looked ready to fall apart at any moment. *Time and distance.* He repeated it over and over in his head, praying for both.

The second he'd seen the arsonist, they'd started to run. Mike and Julia had dashed into the woods, then dropped under a small ridge that emptied out into two paths, both of which led down the mountain. There was no snow on this sheltered section, so it gave them an opportunity to move in a direction that hopefully couldn't be tracked. They chose the path to the right, even though the journey to the bottom would be longer and more treacherous because this eastern route wound in and out of the trees in a confusing zigzag while the other path had been tamped down by years of four-wheelers and snowmobiles. Mike hoped and prayed the arsonist would expect them to take the path of least resistance, and the one closest to the road. Even if that happened, and it bought them a few minutes, the other man would undoubtedly figure it out and cross over to the eastern path. So far, they hadn't heard anyone behind them, but that didn't mean the arsonist couldn't be quieter than two adults who were breathing hard as they trudged through the snowdrifts.

Despite the extra work because of the roundabout path, the area they were walking through was wooded enough to provide a thick cover. The nondeciduous white firs, ponderosa pines and blue spruce crowded up and into each other, mingling with the cottonwoods and aspens, like a blanket of camouflage. On an ordinary sunny day, that might be enough to hide their tracks. But with the snow, they might as well have painted a neon pink path for the arsonist to follow every step they took.

"Ginny, let's fix your coat," Mike said. He bent down and helped a reluctant Ginny out of her coat, then he turned it inside out and re-zipped it, trading the pink fabric for the off-white lining. Then he hoisted his daughter back onto his hip.

Ginny, fragile and small, clung to his neck. He shifted her weight as he moved, stepping hard into the snow to leave a path for Julia that would keep her less protected feet out of the deepest stuff. Even so, he knew they didn't have long before the exposure would cause the beginnings of frostbite in her toes. All he could do was focus on the path ahead of him, not the what-ifs.

Smoke kept billowing into the air to their west. Even from here, he could smell the burning wood of the cabins, and the desperate fear that came with danger that was mere minutes away from them. The heavier the snowfall, the faster it would put out the flames, but hopefully that didn't happen too fast and someone in Crooked Valley spotted the smoke and called for help.

Every so often, either Julia or Mike checked for a cellular signal, but this deep in the woods and this far removed from town, there was nothing. They needed to get farther down the mountain, and they needed to do it now.

Ginny looked up at him. "Daddy, I'm scared."

"I know, Gin, I know." He hugged her tighter, as if that would be enough to save her from what was on their heels. "It's going to be okay, honey. I promise."

He knew he hadn't been the best father, but he vowed that from this moment forward—if God helped them survive—he would do whatever it took to make his daughter's life wonderful again. He would find a way to create the magic that Mary had made so easily, because his daughter needed him more than ever before.

"Why did the bad man try to hurt us?" Ginny asked.

Mike flicked a glance at Julia, but neither of them had an answer. Sometimes there were people in the world who had evil intentions, with reasons that no one else could understand. "I don't know, honey. All we can do is pray that God stops him."

"I'll pray really hard, too, Daddy." Ginny snuggled closer, clutching her bear as tight as he was holding her. Although Ginny's weight was starting to make his arms and back ache, Mike felt safer with her close to him. Besides, her little legs wouldn't be able to keep up with Mike's and Julia's longer legs, and they needed to move quicker than they had been until now.

Because he had just heard something behind them. Something that could have been an animal— or could have been a man who wanted to kill them.

"Did you hear that?" Julia whispered. All Mike could do was nod and speed up his pace. Three of them trying to outrun one person was a difficult task, and the snowstorm working its way through the mountain made that next to impossible. What on earth were they going to do?

*We need help, Lord. Please give me a way to keep my family safe.*

They rounded a grouping of squat, fat spruce trees, and just like that, an opportunity opened up before Mike. An idea formed in his head, and he reacted before he could finish thinking it through. "Take Ginny!" he said to Julia.

"What are you doing?" Julia said as they quickly transferred Ginny.

"Hopefully slowing him down." The sound of someone running, crashing actually, through the woods was still distant, but seemed to get closer by the second. Ahead of them was a stand of fallen trees, all leaning against one broken oak that sat beside the roughed-in semblance of a trail. Thick forest on either side of them would make getting through here a lot more work, if Mike could block the way for the evil behind him. Mike waved Julia and Ginny past the trees, then grabbed one of the branches and pulled, leaning all of his weight into the action. His feet slipped on the snow, nearly throwing him down, but he planted one foot, then the other, leaned back and pulled.

"Mike! Look out!" Julia cried just as the pile of dead trees came tumbling down. They rolled over each other like a pile of bowling balls, hitting the ground with thunderous finality.

At the last second, Mike jumped to the left. The biggest, thickest tree trunk, weighing at least a couple hundred pounds, came crashing onto a sapling, flattening the young, fragile tree and missing Mike by millimeters. His heart hammered in his chest, but he kept running until he reached Julia. "Come on, we have to keep moving."

"You almost got killed," Julia said in disbelief.

"I had to do something. Here, give me Ginny.

Those tennis shoes are too hard to run in already." He took his daughter and clutched her to his chest. He wished he could do the same for Julia. He could see her teeth chattering from the cold and knew every minute they spent outside was a minute she didn't have.

"Daddy, is the bad man gone?" Ginny asked.

"I hope so, honey. Just hold on tight, okay? And let's try to be very quiet for now." She did as he asked, tightening her grip on his shoulders and burying her face in the soft fur of her bear.

It was still at least a mile and a half to the bottom of the mountain, too far for them to make it on foot, not with the storm and Julia in tennis shoes. The tree detour would only slow the other man down for a few minutes, not a few hours. Mike needed another option, but what that option would be, he had no idea.

And then, like another gift from God, an outcropping of rocks appeared between the trees. The snow wasn't as heavy on the rocks, maybe because they'd been warmed by the sun earlier this morning. Either way, the hard surface provided a route that didn't broadcast their every step. He pointed and Julia nodded.

He blazed the way forward, his heavy boots tamping down the snow. Behind him, Julia was struggling to match his long stride. Her feet were probably almost frozen, limiting her movements and affecting her balance. He wished they were closer to the bottom, closer to some kind of civilization, but this small break from the snow would have to do.

Finally, they reached the rocks. Mike and Julia scrambled across them, being careful not to slip as they headed downhill. Then Julia took a step, and he heard the unmistakable screech of the rubber sole of her shoe slipping on the cold, smooth surface of the rock. He lunged forward to catch her, but he was too late. "Julia!"

Julia tumbled down, her arms flailing as she reached for purchase that wasn't there. She stumbled against the edge of the rocks and disappeared a second later.

"Julia!" Ginny screamed.

Mike set Ginny against a tall rock that kept her hidden from anyone coming up behind them. His chest pounded with worry and dread. Julia had to be all right. She just had to. "Stay right here, Gin. Don't move."

"Daddy, is she okay?"

"I'm going to go check on her. Don't move. If you see anything, shout." He didn't want to leave his daughter there, but he couldn't risk dropping Ginny or having her get any closer to the rocky edge. One of the people he cared about being in danger was one too many.

He scrambled over to the ledge and peered over, whispering prayers as he did. Was he too late again? *God, please, no. Let me find her. Let her be all right.*

He leaned a little farther, and then she was there, just a few feet below him, holding her ankle. She had a scrape on her cheek and a tear in her jeans, but she was okay. Thank goodness. "You all right?"

She nodded. "But I think I might have sprained my ankle."

He did a quick survey of the area and saw a narrow path that led down the embankment and over to where Julia sat. "Ginny and I will come down to you. We can skirt around the side. The elevation isn't as high there, but it'll take me a minute. Just wait for me, Julia. Don't be stubborn and try to get up by yourself."

She laughed. That was a good sign, Mike decided. "You know me well. I promise to stay put."

He shot her a grin, and a much-needed moment of levity extended between them. It lasted only a flash of a second before Mike scrambled back onto the rocks and hurried over to his daughter. He had no idea how much distance they had put between themselves and the arsonist, or if the other man had given up his search for them when he'd reached the massive pile of deadwood. Either way, Mike wasn't taking any chances. He hoisted Ginny onto his hip again and made his way down the slope, looking right, left and behind him every few seconds. He didn't hear anything but knew the surface of the rocks, coupled with the winter wind blowing up the mountain, would deaden any sounds behind them. His heart beat out an incessant pounding of *hurry, hurry, hurry.*

When they got down to the ledge, Ginny squirmed out of his arms. "Miss Julia! You're okay!"

"I am. I'm glad to see you, kiddo." She gathered Ginny into a tight hug, then raised her gaze to Mike's. "And to see you."

Something warmed his heart, but there wasn't time to think about or deal with that emotion. They had to get out of here and get to somewhere safe. Somewhere with cell reception so they could call for help. With Julia's injured ankle, they were going to move even slower, and that worried him. What if the arsonist caught up to them? The other man was armed—and enraged. A dangerous combination.

"We're both pretty glad you aren't at the bottom," Mike said. "A slip like that could have broken or dislocated your hip or broken your leg or—"

"Dr. Byrne," Julia said with a nod in Ginny's direction. "I think the smaller humans might not want to hear the graphic medical options."

"Oh yeah. Sorry." There he went again, getting nervous and rambling like a fool around her. "I hate to rush you, but we have to hurry. Let's get you up. Do you think you can stand?"

"There's only one way to find out." She took Mike's outstretched hand and teetered to her feet. She winced.

"You can't walk." What was he going to do? Maybe he could carry Julia and have Ginny walk for a while. They'd move slower. Too slow. He couldn't leave either of them on these rocks to go for help, not in this storm, and not with a man with a gun behind them.

"I can walk, Mike." Her big green eyes met his, sure and determined. "Either way, do I have a choice?"

She was so brave, and so strong, and Mike admired the heck out of that about her. "I can carry you."

Julia shook her head. "You already look exhausted from carrying Ginny and leading the way in this deep snow. I'll be fine. Just give me a sec." She grabbed a long stick to use for stability and brushed off his attempts to help her, telling Mike he literally had his hands full with Ginny, which he knew was true, but it didn't stop him from worrying.

They made their way down the rocks carefully and slowly. Mike held his breath until they reached the soft ground of the forest again.

The unexpected delay had eaten up another fifteen minutes. Each second that passed filled Mike with a sense of urgency. At any moment, he expected the whiz of a bullet going by his head. He kept Ginny against his chest, as hidden as she could possibly be. It wasn't enough because they were all still right here, bright contrasts against the white snow, looking like targets at the county fair.

"We need somewhere to hide," he said, but he saw nothing other than trees and more trees. No caves— not that one would be safe during hibernation season anyway—no little cabins, no homes or sheds. There was nothing on this part of the mountain except more mountain. A heavy feeling of discouragement weighed him down. Were they destined to be gunned down, even after all they had done to try to get away?

Ginny's and Julia's cheeks were red, their breath

frosting in the air. The temperature had to be close to freezing, and only dropping by the hour. "You and Ginny both need to warm up some before we keep going."

"I'm hungry, Daddy," Ginny said. "Are we home yet?"

"Not yet." He closed his eyes and drew in a deep breath. *God, please show us a place to go.*

They walked for a while longer, moving as fast as Julia dared on her sprained ankle, trying their best to leave few tracks. Julia led the way and set the pace, while Mike used his free arm to swish a tree branch across their path, muddling their tracks with the newly fallen snow. He wished he'd thought of that sooner, but when they were running for their lives, no one had time to develop much of a strategy to throw off their pursuer. The steadily falling snow was quickly filling in the swish marks from the branch and erasing all trace of them.

As they got lower, the fog created by the cold snow hitting the warmer ground grew lighter, more like a gauzy veil than a thick sheet now. The afternoon sun was a bright ball in the distance blurred by the constant snowfall, which meant it was probably close to two o'clock. In two, maybe three hours, the sun would set and it would begin to get dark, making it too dangerous to descend the mountain.

As far as Mike could tell, they still had a little over a mile to go. Maybe it was safe to make their way back to the road—wherever that was—and get down sooner. Or maybe the arsonist would find them again and pick them off one at a time. There was no way he was going to let them live, not after they saw him set those fires and not when it was becoming increasingly clear that the arsonist had a personal grudge against them.

Julia stopped and put a hand on Mike's arm. "Wait. I know this place. I've seen it before." She pointed ahead of them. "There's a hunter's blind just through those trees. A bunch of hunters share it and take care of it during the season."

To Mike, the area ahead of them looked like every other square inch of this mountain—full of trees and snow. He didn't dare believe that there was a hiding place just ahead of them. "Are you sure? How do you know about it?"

"Darryl drew it. It was the last drawing he made, and he gave it to me. In that session, he told me all about hunting with his father when he was a little boy and described this place in great detail. Plus, I've been looking at that drawing almost every day for months."

"This is the one I saw hanging in the Grindhouse?"

Julia nodded. Pain flickered in her features at the memory. "His mother picked it up a couple days ago. I had been meaning to bring it to her before that but I just…couldn't. But seeing this now…"

"Is a miracle from Heaven," Mike finished. God had heard their prayers and answered with something amazing. It was a place to rest, regroup and hopefully get warm. Then they could make a plan for getting off this mountain and away from the madman who was hunting them. "Come on. Let's get up there so we can rest and get warm."

"Sounds like a great plan," Julia said, quickening her pace with Mike right on her heels. "It should be just through—"

The sound of a gunshot split the cold, crisp air. The three of them froze. In this storm, there was no way that was a hunter trying to get one last buck before the end of the month. The sound was behind them, but closer than anyone would like.

"Daddy, what was that?" Ginny whispered. "Is it the bad man?"

He couldn't answer his daughter and bring that awful truth to her mind. She was scared enough. All he could do was pray they were hidden before the evil caught up with them. "We have to run," he said to Julia. "Which way?"

"Straight through those trees, and past the one that's bent. It should be right above us then." Julia was hobbling as fast as she could, until sweat was pouring down her forehead and she thought she was going to collapse. But she kept going, keeping pace with Mike and Ginny. Only a hundred yards to go. Now seventy. Fifty.

"I'm going to find you and kill you, Julia Beaumont!" The man's voice carried through the canyon and sent a chill up her spine. He was close. Too close. She wasn't going to make it. And she was going to be the reason Mike and Ginny got hurt, too.

Why did he want to hurt her? Who did she know

that could hold that much hate in his heart? The knowledge that this was somehow personal only made the fear in Julia's chest grow.

"Here, let me help you." Mike wrapped an arm around her waist, taking on most of her body weight on her injured side, helping her move forward. They plowed through the snow, no longer being careful or trying to cover their tracks. He knew they were there.

And he was coming for them.

"You can't hide from me!" the man shouted. "I will find you!"

They reached a thick grouping of trees, so close together they had blocked most of the snowfall. Mike skirted a branch that bent down like a leg into the forest. The three of them leaned against it for a second, winded and breathing heavily. "Where?" he asked.

Julia scanned the woods, but it was dark under the cover of the trees. Maybe she was wrong. Maybe this wasn't the picture Darryl had drawn. Maybe he'd made it all up.

And then, just when she thought she'd imagined everything, she saw it, so subtle she would have missed it if she didn't know it was there. "There it is, just as Darryl described it! See that rope on the side of the tree? Hanging a few feet from the ground? Pull on that and a ladder should come down."

Mike put Ginny down, and Julia wrapped a protective arm around her. "I'll be right back, okay, Gin?"

She nodded, her eyes wide and scared. Julia held the little girl close, while Mike darted across to the other tree, circling it until he found the length of dark green rope. He yanked on it, and a rope ladder unfurled from the hunter's blind to the forest floor. Mike held the ropes steady and waved the girls over.

There was the sound of another shot, this time closer, maybe over the ridge they had just gone over, but far enough away that it seemed like he was only shooting to scare them right now. Mike and Julia exchanged a glance. This was their one chance to hide, to maybe gain an advantage and, most of all, to save their lives. The gravity of the moment wasn't lost on either of them.

"Ginny, I want you to climb this as fast as you can," Mike said, his steady voice not betraying any of the fear he undoubtedly felt. "Like a little monkey. Okay? Julia and I will be coming up right behind you."

"Yes, Daddy." She grabbed the two sides of the ladder, then scrambled up it, nimble and fast.

"You next," he said to Julia once Ginny was at the top. He held the ladder tight and waited for her to get her footing. "Be careful of your ankle."

Julia started up, using her arms to pull her weight, and wincing every time she put weight on her injury, but not letting the pain slow her down. There would be time to nurse her ankle later. Seconds later, she reached the top and slid under the flap and into the blind.

Just in time to see Mike turn and take off in the opposite direction.

"Daddy!"

Julia held Ginny back to keep the little girl from climbing down from the blind and running after her father, fighting the urge to scream at Mike herself. Why would he leave them? What was he doing?

If there was one thing she knew about Mike, it was that he wasn't a man to run from danger. He had a plan, and he was clearly counting on Julia to keep his daughter safe. Julia pulled up the rope ladder before closing the flaps that covered the entrance and the two windows in the blind. Between the camouflage print of the blind and the branches that were attached all over the structure, they should be well hidden from anyone on the ground. She hoped.

"Ginny," Julia whispered, taking Ginny's two mittened hands in her own, "we have to be super quiet."

"I want my daddy." Ginny's eyes filled. "Where did he go?"

"I'm not sure. But I know he's doing what it takes to keep us safe. Our job is to be very, very quiet and stay right here. Can you do that with me?"

Ginny nodded. She sat cross-legged on the floor beside Julia, clutching her teddy bear to her chest. The poor battered stuffed animal was wet and dirty, but Ginny didn't care.

Julia knew from Darryl that the sturdy wooden structure had been soundproofed on the interior, to keep the deer from hearing a hunter load a cartridge, he'd told her, but Julia didn't know how soundproof that meant, so she kept her voice at a whisper. She slipped off her tennis shoes, drew her knees to her chest and covered her legs and feet with her coat.

Underneath the jacket, she rubbed her frozen toes with the warm wool of her mittens, praying for sensation to return.

Every gust of wind and creak of a tree made her heart rate spike. The minutes passed as slowly as a sloth climbing a tree. Julia kept expecting to hear the crack of a gunshot, but the world was quiet. Almost deathly quiet.

Which meant something bad was on its way.

Every cell in Mike's body screamed at him to stay with his family. To climb into the hunter's blind, hold his daughter close and keep them all safe. But hiding would do the opposite, and put them all in danger. As long as that man was out there, none of them could be safe, and that meant he had to do something.

So he ran toward the man with a gun, toward the person who wanted to kill them. He grabbed a big, thick log as he moved. It wasn't a deadly weapon, but it was all he had out here in the wilderness.

Mike had never been a violent man and had never, in fact, even been in a fight in grade school. But this time, he would do what it took to protect his family, even if it meant hurting the person who was determined to hurt them. Mike prayed for strength and calm even as his heart raced and his chest tightened.

The sound of a breaking branch startled him. He darted behind a big tree, pressing himself to the rough bark. He moved an inch at a time until he could peer around the hefty trunk. Oh no. They weren't as far ahead of the other man as they had prayed.

A dusting of snow covered the arsonist's jacket and the hood of his sweatshirt, muting the camouflage colors he was wearing. Whoever it was, Mike didn't recognize him, or the truck he'd been driving.

The sun glinted off the barrel of the rifle the arsonist was carrying, and a shiver of dread ran down Mike's spine. Two hundred yards away, his daughter and Julia were hiding in a hunter's blind, alone and scared. There was no help on the way, no one who could rescue them or stop this madman from shooting them. There was only a determined veterinarian and the man trying to kill them.

"Where are you, Julia?" the man shouted, his voice an angry singsong. "You have to pay for what you've done!"

How did this man know Julia? What on earth had Julia done? And what could possibly make this man so angry at her?

The arsonist kept walking, his steps heavy thuds against the snow. The other man didn't even try to be quiet or hide his path, which meant he knew they were close and didn't care. That showed a level of confidence that could be his undoing, or at least Mike prayed for that.

The other man was fifteen yards away, then ten. Everything Mike cared about was up in that tree, and there was no way he was going to let this criminal threaten that Mike raised the piece of wood over his head and surged around the tree and then forward, swinging the log at the other man's head just as the arsonist turned. Instead of making direct contact, the blow glanced off his shoulder. The arsonist roared with pain and rage. "I'm going to kill you!"

He raised the rifle just as Mike swung up with the log, knocking into the arsonist's hand. The gun discharged, and a deafening boom filled the air, reverberating through the canyon like thunder.

A searing pain raced along Mike's arm, making him drop the heavy wood, but he didn't have time to process what had happened to him or to even acknowledge the wound. He lunged toward the other man, shoving into his chest as he did, knocking the smaller man onto the ground.

Before Mike could pin him down, the man scrambled back and got to his feet. He raised the gun again and pointed it straight at Mike's head. "I'm going to kill you, and then I'm going to kill your little girl and your girlfriend. You all can pay for what she did."

"Why are you doing this?" Maybe Mike could buy some time, get the guy to talk and then find a way to overpower him. The log lay just a few feet away, too far to reach it without risking the man firing. Mike prayed for an answer, prayed for help, prayed for God to protect his daughter and Julia. *Keep him talking, buy some time.*

"Pretty little Julia knows what she did. And she has to pay, just like all the rest of them." He sighted through the barrel of the rifle. "You and your daughter were just in the wrong place at the wrong time."

"Mike!" Cal Moretti's voice came from behind Mike. Far below them, the sound of sirens started, very faint, but growing louder and louder by the second. "Put the gun down, mister, or I'll blow your head off."

The other man flicked a glance in Cal's direction, then backed up two steps, never lowering the gun. "You got lucky, Doc. That's not going to happen again."

Then he was gone, disappearing into the thick woods like a ghost.

# Chapter Nine

Julia and Ginny stayed glued to Mike's side, sitting
on the tailgate of Cal's truck, while the authorities
arrived at the top of Mount Pine and fanned out to
search for the arsonist. Julia had wrapped her feet
in old T-shirts and put on an old pair of Cal's army
boots that had been in the truck. Cal had taken off
the shirt he was wearing and torn the cotton into
strips that he could wrap around Mike's wound while
Ginny sat in Julia's lap and leaned against her father's opposite shoulder. Ginny fell asleep clutching her father with one arm and her well-loved bear
with the other.

"It was a through-and-through." Cal pointed to the
wound. "If it had been a few inches to the right…"

He didn't need to finish that sentence for Julia
and Mike to grasp his meaning. Those few inches
were the distance between the outside of Mike's
arm and the center of his heart. If Cal hadn't come
along when he did, there was no doubt the arsonist

would have killed him. The thought of how close they had all come to never seeing the light of day… Julia couldn't even go there. And all for what? To cover up another fire? To scare them? For what reason? Why on earth had the arsonist followed her all the way up to Mount Pine in the first place, and why was he targeting Julia?

The storm had finally stopped, leaving Mount Pine a white, glistening snow globe. Julia wondered how God could have so much beauty amid such evil. Maybe it was just a reminder that the world was mostly beautiful, and that all this ugliness was temporary.

Or at least it would be once they caught the man.

"What were you doing up here?" Mike asked Cal as he draped his coat over his bandaged arm and clutched the front together.

"You invited me, remember? Told me it would be relaxing." Cal arched a brow and grinned. "I don't know how you define relaxing, but being chased by a homicidal maniac is not it."

Julia and Mike laughed. A part of her felt guilty for the moment of levity when so many serious things had just happened. And when the man who had tried to kill them was still on the run. Even here, surrounded by cop cars, she worried that a bullet might come out of nowhere at any second. So she moved as close to Ginny as she could get, as if she were able to shield the little girl and her father from any more danger.

"I saw the cabin on fire," Cal continued. "Then I

saw your tracks in the snow. I have some training in that, you know, from the military, so I followed you and was lucky to get there just in time."

It *had* been just in time, Julia realized. Was that a miracle from God or a suspicious coincidence? She thought of what Officer Cho had said about the arsonist possibly being former military. Could Cal be working with the stranger who had shot at them?

All she knew was that Ginny, Mike and Julia were together now and out of the woods. Every inch of Julia wanted to hug Mike and make sure he wasn't hurt. She wanted to tell him how terrified she had been when she heard the gunshot, and how she had braced herself for the worst. How her heart had broken for several long seconds while she thought that shot had taken Mike's life.

She had sat in the hunter's blind with Ginny, holding the little girl close, telling her that it would all be okay, when Julia had no idea if anything would ever be okay again. All the while, she'd waited with her heart in her throat, so sure that the next gunshot she heard would be aimed at the blind.

Instead, she had peeked out one of the windows and saw Cal Moretti and Mike heading toward them, almost like a dream. Ginny had scrambled down from the blind, plowing into her father and holding him so tight she nearly knocked him off his feet. It was then that Julia had seen the blood running down Mike's arm and realized how close he had come to dying.

Cal then led the three of them through the woods

and out to his truck, which he'd left parked along the side of the road, just as the police and fire department arrived. Cal explained that he had seen the fire on his way up the mountain, and he'd called the authorities. He'd tried calling Mike when he realized with a panic that the cabin on fire was the one where Mike had been staying. When Cal got no answer, he started off into the woods, looking for his friend. Then he'd heard a gunshot and ran toward the sound—a soldier making sure one of his own came home safe.

The arson investigator arrived, followed by an ambulance. While the fire department battled the blaze farther up the mountain, an EMT checked out Mike and Julia. Ginny woke up for a few minutes for the EMT to check her over, then accepted a granola bar from one of the police officers before climbing into the back seat of Cal's truck and going back to sleep.

"You're all going to be okay," the paramedic told them. "But you're lucky. If you'd been out on this mountain much longer… Anyway, I'm glad Mr. Moretti found you in time."

"I am, too," Mike said. He gave Julia's hand a squeeze and then clapped Cal on the shoulder. "Very grateful."

While the EMT changed out the dressing on Mike's arm, Julia huddled under a wool blanket and sat on Cal's tailgate, too wired and nervous to get inside the cab. The paramedics had checked her ankle, wrapped it with a flexible bandage and then given her several pairs of socks to wear, to help warm her feet gradually, because doing so too quickly could do more damage than good. Already, she could feel sensation returning to her toes. Thank goodness.

She scanned the horizon, half-terrified to see a flash of camouflage or the barrel of a rifle. But there was nothing other than the red of the fire trucks, the gray smoke of a stubborn fire and the dark blue of the officers searching the woods.

The arson investigator stopped to talk with the lead officer on the scene, then crossed to Cal. "You tracked them?" he asked.

"Yes, sir."

Cho's gaze narrowed with suspicion. "Seems awfully coincidental that you were up here the same time as them."

Cal walked Cho through the same timeline he'd given Mike, but Julia could see Cal growing frustrated by the investigator's distrust. "I'm telling you the truth."

"Don't go anywhere," Cho said. "I might have further questions for you." Then he crossed over to Mike and Julia. "Miss Beaumont, Dr. Byrne. I'm sorry to hear about what you all went through. Can you tell me what happened today?"

As quickly and succinctly as they could, Mike and Julia told Officer Cho their version of what had happened. The investigator took notes, only interrupting to clarify a few points. "Did the man in the woods say anything to either of you?"

"He seemed to have some kind of personal vendetta against me," Julia said. "He kept yelling that he was going to kill me. But I have no idea why."

Mike turned to face her. "When it was just him and me, he said he had to make you pay, just like he made the others pay."

"The others?" The investigator flipped through his notepad. "You said you knew Judge Bishop and the attorney…"

"Jim Daly," Julia supplied. "I don't know either of them well. They've been customers once or twice, but I officially met both of them when I testified for the…" Her voice trailed off as the connections began to form in her mind. "The Hinkleys."

"The family whose store was burned down the other day?" Cho asked. The fire chief pulled up, got out of his truck and ambled over to join in the conversation. Cho caught him up, then repeated his question to Julia.

She nodded. "Their son, Darryl, was in a horrific accident a year ago. He had just gotten his license, lost control of the car because he had been drinking, and ended up hitting a telephone pole. Darryl had several broken bones, but his friend died."

"What was this friend's name?"

Julia thought for a second. "Paul…Jameson. I didn't know him, but Darryl talked about him a few times when I was working with him. I was Darryl's occupational therapist."

"That was a horrible accident. I was the commander on the scene that day," the fire chief said. "And what was worse was that Paul was the son of one of our own. I can't even imagine going through that as a parent. Doug Jameson was a wreck after that. Such a tragedy."

"It is." Cho glanced over his notes. "I feel like I'm missing something. Any chance Paul or his family have any connection to any military personnel?"

Mike glanced over at Cal, who was several feet away, talking to another officer. Mike cleared his throat and shifted his weight, clearly uncomfortable. "I don't think this means anything, but my friend Cal was part of a youth ranger camp for a couple years, and he worked with high school kids."

Cho's interest perked. He flipped back a few pages of notes. "Calvin Moretti? He's former military, isn't he?"

"Yeah, but he's the one who rescued us," Mike said. "He has nothing to do with this."

The chief's walkie trilled. "I have to get this."

He moved away to answer the question from his guys. Officer Cho moved a little closer and lowered his voice, clearly trying to keep their conversation private. "You said you met Judge Bishop and Mr. Daly when you testified, Ms. Beaumont. What were you testifying about?"

"The Jamesons wanted Darryl brought up on charges." Julia could still see the devastated family in the courtroom that day. She'd felt so bad for Paul's heartbroken mother, who sat there and sobbed quietly, and for his father, who had screamed at the judge after he made his decision, then blamed the prosecutor for not making a strong enough case. "The Hinkleys said

their son had already lost so much—his football scholarship, his mobility, his friend—and they asked the
judge not to sentence him to actual jail time. I was one
of the character witnesses who testified for Darryl."

"Was Jim Daly the lawyer representing the Hinkleys?"

"Yes." Her eyes widened. She thought of that day
in the courtroom and the rage in Doug Jameson's face.
The same rage she had heard today. But it couldn't be
true. Doug Jameson was supposed to be one of the
good guys, rescuing people from fires, not setting
them. "When Judge Bishop sentenced Darryl to pro-
bation only, Paul Jameson's father started screaming
at the court. He had to be escorted from the courtroom by the bailiff. I think he even got a contempt
charge. It was a chaotic scene."

She could see that the chief doubted the connection between Paul's death and the fires. Even she
doubted a fireman would purposely hurt people.

"Did you know that auto mechanic shop and the
warehouse were properties owned by Judge Bishop?
Jim Daly's office was targeted twice, as was Judge
Bishop's home and the prosecutor's. All three of
those men were also part of a program that got trou-
bled teens to go to the ranger camp you spoke about.
This arsonist had a list, Ms. Beaumont, and you are
clearly one of the people on it. Do you know this
Cal Moretti?"

Mike stepped forward. "He has nothing to do with
this, Officer. I swear. I only mentioned it because

you were asking if any of this had any connection to the military."

"Frankly, Dr. Byrne, I find it highly convenient that Mr. Moretti was here at the same place and time as the man who supposedly set fire to your cabin," Cho said. "How well do you know Cal Moretti anyway?"

"Well enough to know he didn't do this," Mike said. "You're following the wrong path, Officer."

"If not Cal, then who…" Julia didn't need to finish the question because none of them had the answers.

"I'm going to go talk to the fire chief," Cho said. "I'd like to do a follow-up interview with you two tomorrow. For now, go home and get some rest. We'll post squad cars outside your homes and businesses tonight."

"But are we safe, Officer Cho?" Julia asked.

Cho's gaze swept the forest where a dozen police officers were still searching for a killer. "Not yet, Ms. Beaumont. Not yet."

"I think you should go to your sister's house until they find him," Mike said to Julia as they rode back to Crooked Valley in Cal's truck. Ginny had nodded off again and was in the back seat with Julia, while Mike sat up front with Cal. He'd pulled Cal aside for a couple of minutes to tell him privately about the conversation with Cho. Mike could see the anger and annoyance in Cal's face that he was clearly on their suspect list. Mike had reassured him that it was nothing but a coincidence. There was no way his friend was part of something so horrific.

"I have to agree with Mike, which I rarely do." Cal shot him a grin. Once they were off the mountain, Cal's natural good humor had returned.

"See? That's two against one, Julia." The skies had cleared, leaving them with a picture-perfect starlit sky that felt anything but comforting to Mike right now. "It'll be safer with three of you there."

The police hadn't found the man with the rifle before the sun set. He had done a good job of covering his tracks, brushing them away with tree branches or running in circles that confused the landscape. Mike hoped the cops didn't waste too much time pursuing Cal as a lead—time they should be using to catch the man who'd shot at them. Although several officers were still out in the woods of Mount Pine searching, Mike doubted they would find a single trace of the man. He'd been eluding and fooling the firefighters and cops for months and had yet to make a mistake.

That didn't mean he wouldn't do something foolish, because every criminal eventually did. Mike could only pray that the police caught him before anyone else got hurt or any other property was damaged.

He'd called Don Conley and broken the news about his brother's cabin. Don had taken the news in stride, and his only concern was whether Mike and Ginny were safe. Then Mike called Ginny's grandparents, because every time Crooked Valley was on the news for a fire, they worried, and this time, the local stations had mentioned that a "local veterinarian" had been targeted. Where or how the media got that information, he didn't know, but he wanted Ginny's grandparents to hear it from his mouth before they saw it splashed all over the television. There were a lot of questions that Mike did his best to answer, but he was exhausted and overwhelmed with gratitude that they had all made it out alive.

The closer they got to town, though, the more he worried about Julia. Someone had a personal grudge against Julia, and even though that person hadn't hurt anyone yet, he had tried to burn down a house today with them in it. Whatever rage was fueling the arsonist to set these fires wasn't abating, which meant Julia was in even more danger than before. The Crooked Valley Police Department said that officers were going to be stationed outside Judge Bishop's and Jim Daly's houses tonight and had promised to put an unmarked car outside Mike's, Julia's, and Chloe's homes, and do regular patrols of downtown. The PD hoped the arsonist would try again—and not see the undercover cops waiting to catch him.

"I'm not going to stay at my sister's house, Mike," Julia said. "I don't want to put Chloe in danger, or stress her out when she's close to delivering the baby. I know the cops will be outside if I do, but even so, Chloe, Bob and I are basically going to be bait for the arsonist. I can't let her be a part of that danger. Plus, it's almost Christmas Eve. I don't want to ruin that for her."

Mike couldn't let Julia go home to her apartment

alone, though. Even with a policeman outside her door, he worried that she would be too exposed, too much of an easy target. Just as he had in the woods, he felt safer with Ginny and Julia right beside him, and a police presence outside his door. "Then stay at my house. I'm not going to sleep tonight, I can guarantee that. I don't think I'll sleep until they catch him. So why don't you come to my house and take the guest room?"

"I doubt I'm going to sleep, either." She drew the blanket the EMTs had given her tighter around her shoulders. As she did, Ginny began to stir. "I don't want to put you out."

"We've all had a very hard day," Mike said, glancing at Cal, whose face was lined and haggard after another round of questioning, "and I think maybe we should order in some pizza and just forget about everything for a little while. And if you stay at my house, I won't...well, I won't worry about—"

Ginny interrupted before he could finish the sentence. "Daddy, I'm still scared the bad man will come get me."

"You're safe, Gin," Mike said. "I'll be right beside you all night. Why don't we watch a movie with Miss Julia and Uncle Cal and order a pizza?"

"That sounds like the perfect recipe for taking our mind off things, Ginny." Julia smiled at the little girl. "I'd love that."

Mike didn't know whether he should be grateful or frustrated that he'd been cut off before he could admit to worrying about and caring about Julia

Beaumont. Maybe it was too soon. Maybe it was too much. Either way, he hadn't said what he should have said, and next time might be too late.

But maybe it wasn't the right time to tell Julia the truth, not here, with his daughter listening and Cal giving him an amused told-you-so grin. "We have two things to do—pizza and movies," Mike said. "Two very important things. And, Cal, I'm going to need your help to do them."

His friend shot him a teasing glance. "I did save your life today. Doesn't that cancel out anything else on your to-do list?"

"It's a debt I can never repay," Mike said, his voice soft and his throat thick with emotion. If it hadn't been for Cal, he wasn't sure they'd have made it off the mountain. Once again, he wondered how the authorities could suspect Cal at all. He was a good man, a true friend. "But I'll still spend the rest of my life trying."

Cal didn't say anything. For a flames moment, there was only the sound of the tires slapping against the cold tar road. Two men who were rarely vulnerable trying their best not to have a moment. "You've already saved my life, my friend, simply by being there."

"And being stubborn?" Mike grinned, and the heaviness in the cab of the truck lifted. Good thing, because it was about to get emotional.

"*So* stubborn. 'Build me this, Cal. Build me that.'" Cal grinned. "But it's okay because you're a good friend, butterfingers."

"Wasn't my fault. It was a bad pass." The two men laughed at the familiar joke, and the conversation eased into simpler topics as they rode back to Mike's house.

When they arrived, Mike ordered pizza, Ginny took a bath without a second of argument and Julia sat at the table in the kitchen and whipped up a salad. Mike and Cal retrieved boxes from the attic, with Mike doing all the supervising and Cal doing all the lifting. For the first time since Ginny broke her wrist, Mike knew how frustrated his daughter must have felt, unable to do the simplest of things because he'd been ordered not to lift his arm in case it made the wound open up again.

Julia set the salad on the table, then laid out plates and silverware while the men unboxed what Cal had brought down from the attic. "What's all this?"

"The day after tomorrow is Christmas Eve," Mike said, "and I want my little girl to have a Christmas that reminds her the world is mostly good."

And that the world Ginny used to know was still there. That Mike wasn't going to let her down, or ruin the magic. That this Christmas would be different from the ones before, and so would every Christmas to come, but that didn't mean it couldn't be wonderful in its own way.

He vowed to treasure every holiday, every weekend, every moment, that he had with the people he loved. He'd come too close to losing someone again, and there was no way Mike wanted to let a moment pass that wasn't special or heartfelt. Even if that meant opening up and talking about his feelings instead of hiding behind big words and clinical talk.

"I think that's a great idea," Julia said and gave him a smile that gave him a little internal vote of confidence to be more...vulnerable, if that was the right word. Either way, Mike didn't want to ever regret keeping his thoughts to himself again.

Then the doorbell rang, the pizza arrived and everyone dug in, plowing through three large pizzas in a matter of minutes. Mike, Ginny and Julia hadn't eaten since breakfast, and it was as if that first bite unleashed a hunger they didn't even know they'd had.

The four of them traded jokes around the table, with Cal laughing more than Mike had seen his friend laugh in years. Ginny squirmed in her seat, anxious to start the tree. "Daddy, it's almost Christmas. We gotta hurry and get the tree all pretty."

"I agree, Gin. We have waited long enough, haven't we, kiddo?" He gave her a one-armed hug, then got to his feet. "Time to put away dinner and get to work, everyone, as Ginny just reminded me. Gin, can you take your dishes into the kitchen?"

"Yes, Daddy!" She hopped out of her chair and hurried into the kitchen, then rushed back to grab Cal's plate. As nice as it was to hear Cal's laughter, it was even better to see his daughter excited and happy instead of argumentative and grumpy. Inch by inch, Ginny was returning to the little girl who had captured his heart the day she was born.

A few minutes later, the table was cleared and dinner was put away. The adults ambled into the living room while Ginny got her teddy bear from his tumble in the dryer and set him in front of the tree to watch. Although the stuffed animal was dry after his day in the snow, that bear was going to need a sneak bath in the washing machine sometime this weekend. Mike would have to do it while Ginny was asleep, because he was pretty sure she was never going to let go of it after their scare today.

"Let's divide and conquer." Mike handed a box of ornaments to Julia and another to Cal, then took the smaller box of the most precious ornaments for him and Ginny to hang.

"Mike, if you want me to bow out while you guys work on the tree, I understand. I can read or call Chloe or something," Julia said. "A Christmas tree is filled with family memories, and maybe I shouldn't be a part of it. Because I'm not…well, not part of the family."

Here was his out, his opportunity to push away all these feelings of connection with Julia. To erect a wall and keep his heart protected. But as he looked at this woman who had risked her own life to save his life and his daughter's, he knew there was only one answer. "You are already a part of our family and our memories, Julia. I would love it if you were part of this one, too."

She gave him a shy smile and a quiet nod. "I'd be honored."

Their gazes held, and something warm unfurled between them. Something that made Mike want to take risks, to hope for a future again and, most of all, to believe in happy endings.

"All right, enough of this," Cal said, clapping his hands and giving Julia and Mike a side-eye. "You're making this big, strong military guy sick to his stomach with all your mushiness, you two. We have a tree to decorate. Let's get to it."

The words *big, strong military guy* echoed around a fraction of a doubt in Mike's head but he brushed it off. The authorities were wrong about trying to pin this on Cal. Dead wrong.

"Yay!" Ginny reached into the box Mike was holding and picked up an ornament wrapped in tissue paper.

"Careful, Ginny. Your mom made that one." Mike unrolled the paper and held the delicate ceramic bell by its string. "Make sure you hang it on a strong branch."

"Mommy made this one?" Ginny cupped it in her hands and turned it over, studying the painted holly berries and branches along the base.

"Yup. She took a class the year you were born and made all kinds of ornaments. Some of them she made special because she knew you were coming." As they worked on the tree, Mike told Ginny the story about each of the ornaments her mother had created and collected. This time, the memories didn't sear his heart as they had the Christmas before, when he'd stopped decorating the tree after a handful of ornaments and spent a solid week unable to look at anything Christmas. This time, telling Ginny about the wooden cradle ornament Mary had made for her newborn daughter or about buying the sailboat ornament on a trip to Florida with Mary filled him with a warm joy, not pain. Ginny asked questions and opened up conversations they hadn't had over the last eighteen months. His late wife's memory came to life in that room, and to Mike, it felt as if Mary was smiling down on this new normal that Mike was beginning to carve out with his daughter and two very special people in his life. Ornament by ornament, the bare tree began to sparkle and shimmer with Christmas spirit.

Eventually, the long day caught up with his daughter. Ginny lasted through a few more decorations before she started yawning. "Uncle Cal, I'm tired. Can you read me a story?"

"Sure, kiddo. Go pick out a book." Cal settled into the big recliner in the corner of the living room. Ginny gathered a pile of books from the bookcase beside it, then climbed into his lap. Before the last page of *Where the Wild Things Are*, Ginny had fallen asleep. "Looks like we have a quitter here."

Mike chuckled and scooped his daughter into his arms, once again overcome by gratitude that they were all safe and at home. He knew the arsonist was out there —somewhere—but with the cruiser in front and all of them together, Mike felt like he could breathe a little easier. "I'll tuck her into bed."

Cal got to his feet and pressed a kiss to his goddaughter's forehead. "I'm going to hit the road myself. Merry Christmas, Mike, Julia."

"Sure you don't want to stay?" Mike asked. "I could use another stud around here."

Cal grinned. "That presumes you already have one stud, Mr. Nerdy Vet. The cops will be here to keep an eye on you and I feel good about that. But if you want me to come back, just say the word, Mike."

"Thank you, Cal," Julia said. "Those two words don't seem like nearly enough to say for what you did today, but please know how grateful I am that you were there and that you saved Mike from…" Her eyes filled and she paused a second. "Saved us all."

"It was nothing," Cal said, his face red, clearly uncomfortable with the praise and emotion. "Thanks for the pizza, Mike."

"Anytime. I mean it, Cal. Anytime." The two men exchanged a look of friendship and solidarity, then Mike headed down the hall with his sleeping child.

After Mike was gone, Cal turned back to Julia. "Take care of him. He might be a pain in the neck, but he's the nicest pain in the neck I know."

"I have to agree." Her gaze went to where Mike had gone, and everything inside her softened. This man who had come into the coffee shop and asked her to do the impossible had grown on her in a lot of ways. She'd come so close to losing him today, and in those tense, horrible minutes inside the hunter's blind, she'd realized that she might just be falling in love with the handsome veterinarian.

"I think you kind of like him," Cal said.

"I do." For years, she had kept her emotions under a tight lock and key. The painful end to her marriage, the death of Darryl—all of it had left her reluctant to be vulnerable, to care about another and, most of all, to allow someone else into her heart and then let them down when they needed her most. "To be honest, Cal, I more than like Mike."

A smile lit Cal's face. "Good. Because he deserves to be loved again, and from all I've seen of you in this short time I've known you, I'd say you do, too."

His words warmed her. She liked this gruff military man who was really a big softie under all his bluster and brawn. The suspicion of the authorities that Cal was somehow involved seemed wrong in so many ways. This was a good man, not a killer. "Thank you. And I'd say the same to you." She took one of his hands in her own. "I know I keep saying this, but I mean it. Thank you, Cal, for all you did for us today. I don't know what I would have done if I'd lost Mike or Ginny."

"Me, too." He cleared his throat, then fished in his pocket for his keys, avoiding eye contact. But not before Julia saw the glimmer of a tear in the tough man's eyes. "See you around."

After Cal left, Julia checked to see that the cruiser was still in place before she took a seat on the otto man just as Mike came back into the room. All of a sudden the silence in the house seemed deafening. It was just the two of them and the soft light of the Christmas tree and a whole lot of words no one was speaking. Julia felt like she had a thousand things to say to him—and a thousand reasons not to say any of them.

"So...uh, how about I put on some music and we can finish decorating the tree?" He shifted his weight from side to side, and a flush filled his cheeks. Maybe she wasn't the only one feeling uncomfortable now that it was just the two of them. "You don't have to stay if you've changed your mind, I just...well, as ridiculous as it sounds, I don't want the day to end."

Joy flickered in her heart. "Neither do I. I'd like to stay, Mike. Very much."

A smile spread across his face, and all that silence from a moment ago seemed to disappear. "Excellent." He pulled out his phone, opened a music app and connected it with Bluetooth to the stereo to play some Christmas music.

Julia started humming along with "Joy to the World," and Mike joined in with his rich baritone. All of tonight had been magical, a moment that Julia knew she would forever treasure. If nothing ever came of this—whatever this was with Mike—that would be okay, because she would hold on to the memory of tonight for the rest of her life.

"All we have left to do is put up the angel," Mike said, reaching into the box and pulling out a porcelain angel with gossamer wings. "I usually let Ginny put the angel up, but she's out like a light after everything that happened today. As the honorary member of the Byrne family tonight, would you like to do the honors?"

Honorary member? She liked the sound of that. But then she thought of all the memories he had shared with his daughter as they hung the ornaments and how hard it must have been for him to include another woman in the place where his wife had once stood. Maybe Mike wasn't as ready to move on as Cal thought. "Mike, this is your tree, your memories with Ginny and your wife. If this all feels weird, I get it. I do."

"I'm creating *new* memories with you, Julia. You're as much a part of today as everyone else." He handed her the delicate figurine. His brown eyes held nothing but honesty. "You protected my daughter with your own life. This is my way of saying thank you."

A fissure of disappointment ran through her. For a second, she'd thought he was as moved by the moment as she had been, that he was falling for her, too, but it was all a thank-you. Nothing more. She was a fool to let her heart get swept up in this moment and to think there was something deeper brewing between them. She forced a smile to her face. "Of course, Mike. Ginny is a wonderful girl, and I'm glad I was there."

Instead of accepting the angel, she averted her gaze and tugged her phone out of her pocket, swiping quickly to an app. "Gosh, it's so late. I'm going to call an Uber. I really should go home. I'll let the police department know, and they'll send someone to watch over me, so you don't have to worry."

She needed to get out of here before she fell too hard for Mike. In the back of her mind, she knew the arsonist was still searching for her, and even though the cruiser had given her a momentary sense of protection, it would be best if she was far away from Mike and Ginny so they could be safe.

"If you're determined to go, I won't stop you," Mike said. A note of disappointment hung in his words. He set the angel on an end table and then thumbed toward the kitchen. "But are you sure you don't want to stay and help finish getting the house ready for Christmas?"

If she stayed another moment, she knew her heart would break. Another memory, another connection, another realization that they were only friends. This was for the best. It was the safest option for all of them. And for her heart. "Maybe some other time." She slipped into her coat and reached for the door handle. Just before she turned the knob, two things happened—Julia heard a loud bang and then noticed something familiar and terrifying through the glass.

A red pickup truck parked at the end of his street. A red pickup truck she had seen chasing them down the mountain road today. A red pickup that could only mean one thing. He had followed her here and was going to hurt them again.

The cruiser still sat in the street, but no one was behind the wheel. A dark puddle lay in the street beside the driver's side door, visible under the streetlight. Oh no. "Mike, he's here."

Mike rushed to her side and peered out into the darkness. He went rigid and still. "We have to call the police."

"Where's the officer that's supposed to be here

watching over us?" Julia asked. "I don't see him in his car."

"I don't know. Maybe they're on a shift change or—"

The sound of breaking glass came from the back of Mike's house, followed by a ball of flames arcing into the kitchen. Mike ran toward the fire, grabbing a blanket from the couch as he did. He threw it onto the flame, smothering the fire before it could spread.

At the same time, Doug Jameson reached inside the broken window and unlocked the back door. He stepped into the kitchen, holding his rifle in one hand and a burning Molotov cocktail in the other. He had the same fury in his face as he had that day in court when the judge had gone easy on Darryl.

"Watch out!" Julia screamed.

Jameson's attention diverted for a split second in Julia's direction. Mike scrambled to his feet and lunged forward, knocking Jameson to the floor. The rifle skittered to one side and the Molotov cocktail to the other, rolling toward the cabinets, the flames on the rag hungry and gnawing at the wooden doors. Julia yanked up the blanket and covered the flames just as they hit the varnished wood.

Jameson scrambled out of Mike's grasp and dove for the gun, knocking Julia into the hard wooden cabinets. She let out a cry of pain.

Mike grabbed Jameson's shirt, hauling him back, but Jameson was like a wild animal, clawing at the floor, trying to get to Julia. "That boy killed my son! You made sure he got off scot-free!" Jameson screamed at her as he thrashed and fought, trying to kick Mike's bigger, heavier body off.

The acrid smell of smoke began to drift into the kitchen through the open back door. Out of the corner of her eye, Julia saw flames dancing across the porch. It was the cabin nightmare all over again, and for a second, Julia was frozen, trapped by her fear of the flame.

Mike grunted as he wrapped an arm around Jameson's neck in a choke hold. "Julia! Put the fire out! I've got him!"

"I...I can't." Terror kept her rooted to where she was.

"Julia, you can. Just—"

Jameson took advantage of Mike's momentary distraction to flip over and slam a fist into Mike's temple. Julia gasped. "Mike!"

The flames were growing, and as much as Julia wanted to rush to Mike's side, she jerked into action and did as he said, grabbing the blanket and running for the back door. Jameson reached out as she passed him. He grabbed her injured ankle and yanked her down to the floor. She twisted and tumbled into the corner. Searing pain raced up her ankle. Three feet away, Mike lay still and quiet. Too still. "Mike?"

Jameson's face curled into a sneer. "I am going to make you suffer! That's all I've ever wanted is for all of you to suffer like he did."

Jameson grabbed his rifle as he rose and loomed over Julia. He raised the barrel and sighted the gun on her chest. There was nowhere to go. Walls on two sides, and Jameson standing before her. Julia curled into a protective ball and prayed. Behind Jameson, she could see Mike slowly get to his feet. In a move that surely came from his high school football days, Mike tackled Jameson to the floor, pinning him in place with one knee.

Jameson thrashed from side to side, but it did no good. Mike's body weight kept him in place. "Someone has to pay!"

Just then a pair of Crooked Valley police officers came running up the back steps. They burst into Mike's kitchen and, in seconds, had Jameson in their grasp.

"Someone already did pay," Julia said softly as the cops put handcuffs on Jameson. Darryl's guilt had been too big of a burden for the teenager to hold, and he had seen no other way out but to end his own life, too. There had been so much pain from this one accident, for both families and for everyone affected by the fires.

The fire department arrived in a whirl of sirens and quickly put out the fire that thankfully had been contained to the deck. One officer read Jameson his rights while another took the rifle and bagged it as evidence. In minutes, it was over, and except for a pair of scorch marks on the kitchen floor and wooden decking and one broken windowpane, it was as if nothing ever happened. Ginny, exhausted by the day, slept through the whole thing.

Julia and Mike stood on the back porch and watched as Doug Jameson was put into the back of a police car. Red and blue lights strobed in the alley. It seemed as if the entire Crooked Valley Police Department was there, along with Officer Cho and the fire chief. There was no victory in capturing Jameson, only a sense of loss that one of their own could go so wrong.

"My son's life mattered!" Jameson shouted before they shut the cruiser's door. "He mattered!"

All Julia could say was, "I'm sorry." For the pain this family must have been in to cause Doug to act out in such a vicious way, for the people who had been hurt in his one-man quest for justice and, most of all, for the guilt that had plagued Darryl and ultimately cost him his life.

"We all are," Mike said and drew Julia into a hug.

# Chapter Ten

Mike woke up bright and early Christmas morning to Ginny bouncing on the bed. She'd slept through everything that had happened three nights before, but Mike had tossed and turned. He was grateful his daughter's happy bubble hadn't been broken, that Doug Jameson was behind bars and Cal's name had been cleared, but he knew it would be a long time until he felt safe again. That harrowing day on Mount Pine, and how close Jameson had come to burning down everything that mattered to Mike, haunted the edges of his thoughts.

"It's so early, Gin." Mike groaned. "Let me sleep ten more minutes."

"Daddy!" Ginny shouted while she clambered all over him. "It's Christmas! Come on, you gotta wake up!"

He rubbed his eyes and moved into a sitting position. Every muscle in his body ached from the events of the other day, but those pains were followed by a fierce wave of appreciation that they had survived and that God had kept everyone safe. He gathered Ginny in his arms and pressed a kiss to her temple. It was Christmas, a day Mike hadn't been sure they would see seventy-two hours ago. "Merry Christmas, Ginster."

"Merry Christmas, Daddy." She snuggled into him for a second, then popped up again. "Can we open presents now?"

Mike chuckled. "Sure. But first, coffee."

Just the word *coffee* made him think of Julia Beaumont. What was she doing this morning? Undoubtedly, she was spending the holiday with her sister and brother-in-law. She'd gone to their house the other night, now that the threat of Jameson was gone.

On his way to Mike's house, Jameson had attacked a neighbor who was walking his dog, beating the man so badly that he started screaming for help. The police officer who had been assigned to guarding Mike and Julia stepped out of his car when he heard the shouts, thinking it might be one of them. That had been enough of a distraction for Jameson to get a single shot off, hitting the officer in the side. The officer had managed to call for backup, thank goodness. He was out of surgery and expected to make a full recovery. The bullet had narrowly missed his kidney.

After the police left with Jameson in the back of a cruiser, Julia called her sister's husband to pick her up and take her to Chloe's for the night. Almost as soon as she left, Mike had noticed her absence in the house. He'd set the angel on the top of the tree, then stared at it for a long time. Was he really going to be that foolish and lose this woman because he couldn't tell her how he felt?

He'd thought he was ready to say how he felt that night, but then the moment had gotten swept up into all the danger and commotion, and once again, Mike had used that as a reason to keep his feelings to himself instead of opening his heart. Was it too late? Was he imagining that Julia might feel the same way?

He texted her, Merry Christmas, waited a beat for a reply then figured she was probably still sleeping, since Julia didn't have a six-year-old bouncing on her stomach at way-too-early in the morning. Mike got dressed and sent Ginny off to wash her hands while he started a pot of coffee. The dark, rich brew percolated and Ginny darted around the living room, peeking at the presents he'd ordered online a couple weeks ago.

"I wanna open this one first. No, this one!" She pointed at one present, then another. She cocked one hip to the side and rested her chin on her hand. "Hmm…maybe this one."

He chuckled. "I promise we will open all of them. But first," Mike said, "I want to tell you a story about Mommy and me."

While he'd tossed and turned last night, he'd thought about everything that Julia, Don Conley and the therapist he had sent Ginny to last year had told him about the importance of keeping her mother's memory alive, talking about the hard times and celebrating the good times. Ginny needed to process her grief, too, and not helping her address that was only causing a deeper divide between them. Telling Ginny the stories behind the precious ornaments had been a step in the right direction. If he took enough of those steps, maybe he could help them both navigate any more rough waters that arose.

"A story about Mommy? Can Bear-Bear listen?" Ginny grabbed her raggedy teddy bear from the kitchen chair and held him to her chest.

"Bear-Bear has been here since the day you were born, Ginny. Of course he can listen."

She grinned, then propped the stuffed animal against a recliner. Mike sat down with Ginny on the floor beside the tree. The lights flickered, dancing a rainbow of colors over Ginny's features. "You probably don't remember your very first Christmas, but I do."

She shook her head. "I was too little, huh, Daddy?"

"You were just six months old, and still a teeny, tiny baby. Your mom was so excited about your first Christmas, though. She wrapped all kinds of presents and baked cookies and did so many decorations. I told her you wouldn't remember any of it, so why would she go to all that work? And do you know what she said?"

Ginny shook her head.

Mike could still see Mary, sitting in this very room beside a different tree, her face kind and patient and beautiful. "She said that she wasn't doing all that work just to make your Christmas magical.

She wanted all three of us to start our family off with wonderful memories about snow and angels and a—"

"Christmas tree! Mommy loved the Christmas tree."

"Exactly. I didn't realize what she was doing back then, and I have to admit that I complained about doing all those decorations. But I am glad now because I have all these memories that I can share with you." Memories he would share more often, of the small moments, and of the big ones, so that Ginny never forgot the amazing woman who had been her mother. "I can tell you about the peanut butter cookies she made that turned out terrible because she forgot the sugar, and I can tell you about how she and I decorated that little magnolia tree outside your bedroom window with twinkling lights so that you could see them if you woke up at night. I can tell you that your mommy did all of those things because she loved you more than she ever loved anything in the world. And I..." He could feel the emotion welling in his chest, rising like a storm surge. The old Mike, the one who had kept everything on a tight leash, would have pushed the feelings away and left the room or changed the subject. But this Mike, who had almost lost everything, leaned into the feelings, let the wave hit him and let all of it show on his face. "I loved her so much, and I didn't tell her enough. I don't want to make that mistake with you, Ginny. I don't want you to wonder for one second if I love you. Because I do. I love you to the moon and back, and I have from the first second I saw you. You, my darling little monkey daughter, are the best part of me and of Mommy."

"I love you, too, Daddy." Ginny climbed into his lap and laid her head against his chest. If Mike had to make a top-ten list of best moments in his life, this one would rank right up there.

Mike reached out and grabbed the teddy bear and dragged his furry body into the circle. "Bear-Bear should be part of this, too. He's had a rough couple of days."

"I think he needs a bath, Daddy." Ginny wrinkled her nose.

"I agree." Mike laughed and hugged her even tighter. "Let's open presents while Bear-Bear takes a spin in the washing machine. Okay?"

With an overly excited first grader, the whole process of opening gifts took like nine and a half seconds. Each moment was worth it, though, to see the joy on Ginny's face and to hear the house filled with happiness and laughter again. It had been far too long since they'd had that. While Ginny played with a new doll, Mike sipped his coffee and watched light snow fall across Crooked Valley.

And wondered what Julia Beaumont was doing and how she had invaded his heart so easily.

The house seemed empty, even with Ginny running back and forth, playing with her toys. Mike knew exactly what they were missing, and he'd be a fool to wait one more second to bring that into their lives. "Gin? Why don't you go get your coat?"

"Where are we going, Daddy?"

"It's a Christmas surprise." He tapped her on the nose. "But you have to hurry before it gets too late."

His daughter scrambled into her coat, tucked her new doll into one of the pockets then waited for Mike to get ready, too. He called a rideshare since his SUV was at the shop getting new tires and some bodywork repaired from the fire damage, then headed for Julia's sister's house. She was just coming outside as he pulled up. He parked in the driveway, got out of the car then stood there like an idiot. "Hey."

"Hey," she said. "Merry Christmas."

"Where are you going?" Okay, so maybe he needed to work on his small talk skills a little bit. Or a lot.

"I was going home. My Uber is on its way," she said, while Mike opened the back door and unbuckled a very excited Ginny. "Why are you guys here?"

"Because we have a Christmas surprise!" Ginny said.

"A Christmas surprise?" Julia cocked her head. "For me?"

"Uh-huh." Ginny nodded. "Daddy didn't tell me what it is, though, cuz it's a surprise."

Julia's rideshare car pulled into the driveway. Any second now, Julia would be on her way, and Mike would miss his chance. He drew in a deep breath. "We want you to be part of our Christmas, Julia. Will you come with us on a very special errand? I can't tell you what it is yet because"—Mike winked at Ginny—"Santa has given me very strict directions."

Julia laughed. "Why not? I'm game. But let me just let the driver know and give him a generous tip for coming out here on Christmas Day." A moment later, she climbed in their Uber, while Mike buckled Ginny into the booster seat.

He was tight-lipped as they drove through Crooked Valley before pulling up to a small ranch-style house in a tidy neighborhood. "Santa said we have to come here this morning and make a very important decision," Mike said. "And we have to do it all together. Okay?"

Ginny squealed with excitement as Mike unbuckled her. The three of them walked up the walkway, and before Mike could ring the bell, Harriet Nichols opened the door. She gave Mike a knowing smile, because he'd texted her just before he left the house to ask if she would help him surprise his daughter. "Merry Christmas, Dr. Byrne. Merry Christmas, Ginny. And Merry Christmas, Julia."

"Merry Christmas, Harriet." He grinned, then held the door while Julia and Ginny went into the house. "Where are they?"

Harriet nodded toward a playpen in the dining room. "Right over there, just waiting for you."

Mike hoisted Ginny on his hip and took Julia's hand. Her hand felt right in his, as if she'd been designed to be beside him. Even after such a short period of time, he couldn't imagine Julia being anywhere else.

"What important decision are we making, Daddy?"

"We're adding to our family, and I think that's something that everyone needs to have input on." Still holding Julia's hand, Mike crossed to the playpen, then set Ginny on the floor. Five adorable black-and-white kittens were tumbling all over each other while their exhausted mother sat on a cat bed in the corner. "Which one is going to be our Christmas kitten?"

Ginny gaped at him. "Daddy, we're getting a kitten?"

"We are indeed." It was time for a new pet in their house, a new life and a new beginning. "But only if we all agree. Adding a pet to a family is a really big decision, and we have to make sure we all love whichever kitten we choose."

"Mike…I…" Julia flushed. "I shouldn't…well, I'm not…"

"Yes, you are, Julia, which is why I couldn't make this decision without you." He turned to her. Harriet had quietly come over to distract Ginny by letting her hold a kitten, giving the adults a moment to talk candidly. It was far past time Mike said all the words he'd kept locked inside himself. "I spent most of my life not telling people how I felt. Not expressing my emotions or what fills my heart. On the day that Mary passed away, she told me she loved me as she was heading out the door, and I just nodded. Even though I loved her, I didn't tell her, because I grew up in a house where being emotional made you vulnerable and weak. All that silence did was leave me with guilt and regret. I don't ever want to let another minute go by without saying what I feel. In private, in front of other people, I don't care." He took both her hands in his and met her gaze. "I love you, Julia Beaumont."

"You…you love me?" She stared at him. "But… how… We…"

Harriet nudged her. "You're supposed to say you love him, too."

He could see Julia's hesitation, her fear of taking a risk, of hurting someone again. He knew those feelings too well. Together, they could begin to heal, to build a life that embraced their losses but also made room for a fresh, joyous start. "Take a risk, Julia. There's too much life to live for you to sit on the sidelines."

She swallowed hard. Beside them, the kittens had noticed the humans and began mewling for attention. Ginny was snuggling the smallest kitten, her face buried in its soft fur. And Mike simply stood there, still holding Julia's hands, his heart lodged somewhere deep in his throat, waiting for her answer.

"I've loved you since that day in the woods," she said softly, her eyes wide and earnest and locked on his. "When you risked your life for us. I knew then that you were the kind of man I could trust with my heart, too. I've just been so afraid of hurting someone else, or being hurt."

How he understood that overwhelming urge to just stay in a little shell, protected from the dangers of the world. But in the end, that shell was nothing but a cage, keeping them from enjoying all the amazing moments God had waiting. "Yesterday taught me a lesson I should have learned a long time ago. The only time we have, Julia, is right now. We should make the most of it." He gave her hands a squeeze and shifted closer to her. "Together. As a family."

A smile curved across her face. "That's all I've ever wanted, Mike. For this Christmas and every single one to come." She stepped into his arms, and he kissed her, light and sweet, a promise for a forever. "Well, and maybe a kitten, too."

"Can we get two, Daddy?" Ginny said as she held up two tiny balls of fur at the same time. "And then when I have a little sister someday, she'll have a kitten, too."

"A little sister, Ginny?" Mike arched a brow, then glanced at Julia. She smiled and nodded, and the heart he'd always thought was made of steel turned straight into mush.

# Epilogue

Henry Rathburn ran around the Crooked Valley park, chasing a very active and very happy Scotty, whose wheels slid easily over the tar path. His mother watched from the sideline with a smile on her face. "Thank you, Dr. Byrne."

"It was nothing," Mike said. "Truly."

"To one little boy and his dog, that cart you had Cal build was everything." Henry's mother thanked him again, then headed across the park to catch up with her son. Dozens of other Crooked Valley residents milled about the area, talking to Keesha and Jamie, who were manning a booth flanked by two temporary pens.

When Mike had asked Ginny what she wanted for her birthday, she said she wanted everyone she knew to have a kitten—or a puppy—so Mike had decided to combine her party with an adoption event, something that was long overdue for the animals of Crooked Valley. So far, half of the animals they had brought to the event had found homes, and judging by the number of people standing by the pens, every single one would find a family today, just like the two feisty kittens at his own house.

Cal Moretti was chatting with Don Conley at a picnic table, probably comparing notes from high school games they'd each played. Mike nodded a hello before crossing to another table. Seven pink balloons were attached to one end of the table beside a birthday cake big enough to feed a small country. Ginny, the birthday girl, had forgotten about the presents and piñata once she saw Chloe and Bob arrive with their son, Allen, who was six months old and growing like a weed, as Chloe said. Ginny was utterly fascinated with the baby and had started a one-child campaign for a sibling soon after Allen's arrival.

"How's my wife?" Mike said to Julia. She was radiant in a bright pink sundress, with her hair piled in a messy bun on top of her head. Even though it didn't seem possible, he could swear she got more beautiful by the day.

"I'm great because my husband is here." She rose on her toes and pressed a kiss to his lips. "And he isn't sick of me after a few months of marriage."

"Never," he whispered in her ear. "Because I'm madly in love with you."

She giggled and kissed him again. They shared a moment of silly, giddy love, then Julia paused and her face sobered. "Wow. They came."

Mike turned to see Darryl Hinkley's parents crossing the park lawn. In the months since Doug Jameson's arrest, Julia had reached out several times to Darryl's parents, to talk about the past and try to find a new present. In that common ground of tragedy, they'd rebuilt their friendship. Still, when Julia invited them to Ginny's birthday party, she had worried that they wouldn't come, that it was too soon, too much.

"Hi, Julia and Mike," Sheila Hinkley said, her face friendly and open. She handed Mike a gift bag. "I know you said no gifts, but Joe and I thought it would be nice to give Ginny something for the animals."

He peeked inside and saw a bag of treats and several toys for dogs and cats. Always a welcome donation for the shelter and something Ginny would undoubtedly delight in giving to the animals. "Thank you. That was very thoughtful of you."

"Well, we think this event is a great idea." Joe Hinkley looked around the park and nodded his approval. "It's a nice way to bring some happiness back to this town after everything that's happened."

Mike glanced at Julia. She gave him a little nod. "If you two have a second, Julia and I have someone we'd like you to meet."

When Mike and Julia had talked about the final details for the rescue/birthday event last week, they'd had an idea that was probably foolish and likely to backfire, but Mike was willing to risk it.

"Someone you'd like us to meet?" Sheila asked, confusion knitting her brows. "We know just about everyone in town."

"This resident doesn't have a permanent address," Julia said with a hopeful smile. "Yet. We were hoping you guys could help with that." She took Mike's hand, and they led the Hinkleys over to where Keesha and Jamie were standing.

Sheila glanced at Joe, then back at Julia. "What's going on?"

Julia took a deep breath. "I know you talked about getting Darryl a dog after his accident. Something that could keep him company, give him motivation to keep moving forward with his therapy, but you never got the chance to do that," she said. "I also know it's been incredibly difficult for the two of you since he died, but that doesn't mean you can't keep that promise. And give you both a reason to keep moving forward."

Mike clipped a leash on the one dog that he'd said was not available for adoption, the one he'd met last week at the Crooked Valley Animal Shelter. A six-year-old chocolate Lab who loved long walks as much as he loved napping in front of the fireplace. A good dog whose owner had died, a tragedy that had left the poor Lab confused and lonely.

"Meet Hunter," Mike said to the Hinkleys. "His owner passed away a couple weeks ago, and he's been struggling ever since."

Joe Hinkley bent down and reached out a hand to

pet the dog. Hunter's tail started wagging, tentative and unsure. "Hey, boy."

Mike couldn't read Sheila's face. For a second, he was sure she was going to yell at him and storm off, but instead her face softened and she pressed a hand over her heart. "It's like you read our minds. Joe and I were just talking about a dog this morning. Not to replace Darryl, because nothing can replace our son, but to sort of honor his memory and, yes, get us both out of the house and off the couch." She bent down beside her husband and scratched the Lab behind one ear. "You lost your person, too, huh, Hunter?"

Hunter cocked his head, listening to these new but friendly voices. Little by little, as Sheila and Joe kept petting him and talking to him, Hunter lowered his guard and inched closer to them until finally he had his whole body pressed against two people who had already fallen in love with him.

"You did a good thing there, Dr. Byrne," Julia said to her husband as they walked away a few minutes later. "And did I see you shed a tear when the Hinkleys signed the adoption papers for Hunter?"

"I wasn't crying. You were crying." He had indeed gotten a little emotional when he'd seen the lost dog finding a home with two people who had an aching hole in their lives. That love between animal and person was part of what made him go into veterinary medicine, and one of the best parts of his job.

"We were both crying," Julia said. "We're turning into a couple of softies."

"Not you. You're the strongest woman I know." She'd been so brave that day in the woods, so selfless. Everything about Julia was about other people, and very rarely about herself. She was kind and compassionate, smart and funny, and best of all, she was also now his wife.

She wrapped her arms around his and leaned against his shoulder, the two of them just watching the people they loved talking and laughing and enjoying the day. "Did I tell you I got a new patient?"

"You did? That's great." Julia had eased her way back into occupational therapy work, starting with adults and then opening her practice to include children again. Chloe and Julia had hired a couple more people to work at Three Sisters Grindhouse, giving Chloe time with her baby and Julia time to spend with her patients. So far, the balance between the two jobs seemed like a good choice for all of them.

"He's ten, and he has a broken leg, and his mother says he's got an attitude." She grinned at Mike. "I think I can handle that."

"If you can handle this difficult and stubborn veterinarian, you can handle anyone."

"You are neither of those things, my darling husband. But you are"—her eyes sparkled and a wide smile took over her face, the kind of smile that made him happy in every single cell of his body, a joy he didn't think could get any bigger or brighter "going to be a wonderful daddy. Again."

"Again?" Mike had been wrong. That joy in his

heart was meant to multiply, and as he took his wife in his arms and placed a hand over the tiny life that was growing between them, he thanked God for giving him a second chance at forever.

\* \* \* \* \*

**Inspired by true events,**
***The Secret Society of Salzburg***
**is a gripping and heart-wrenching story of
two very different women united to bring
light to the darkest days of World War II.**

Don't miss this thrilling and uplifting page-turner
from bestselling author

# RENEE RYAN

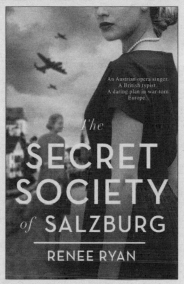

"A gripping, emotional story of courage and strength,
filled with extraordinary characters."
—*New York Times* bestselling author **RaeAnne Thayne**

**Coming soon from Love Inspired!**

**LoveInspired.com**

LI42756BPA

# Get 4 FREE REWARDS!

**We'll send you 2 FREE Books plus 2 FREE Mystery Gifts.**

**FREE** Value Over **$20**

Both the **Love Inspired®** and **Love Inspired® Suspense** series feature compelling novels filled with inspirational romance, faith, forgiveness and hope.

---

**YES!** Please send me 2 FREE novels from the Love Inspired or Love Inspired Suspense series and my 2 FREE gifts (gifts are worth about $10 retail). After receiving them, if I don't wish to receive any more books, I can return the shipping statement marked "cancel." If I don't cancel, I will receive 6 brand-new Love Inspired Larger-Print books or Love Inspired Suspense Larger-Print books every month and be billed just $6.49 each in the U.S. or $6.74 each in Canada. That is a savings of at least 16% off the cover price. It's quite a bargain! Shipping and handling is just 50¢ per book in the U.S. and $1.25 per book in Canada.* I understand that accepting the 2 free books and gifts places me under no obligation to buy anything. I can always return a shipment and cancel at any time by calling the number below. The free books and gifts are mine to keep no matter what I decide.

Choose one:  ☐ **Love Inspired**
Larger-Print
(122/322 IDN GRHK)

☐ **Love Inspired Suspense**
Larger-Print
(107/307 IDN GRHK)

Name (please print)

Address                                                                                          Apt. #

City                                        State/Province                          Zip/Postal Code

**Email:** Please check this box ☐ if you would like to receive newsletters and promotional emails from Harlequin Enterprises ULC and its affiliates. You can unsubscribe anytime.

> **Mail to the Harlequin Reader Service:**
> **IN U.S.A.:** P.O. Box 1341, Buffalo, NY 14240-8531
> **IN CANADA:** P.O. Box 603, Fort Erie, Ontario L2A 5X3

**Want to try 2 free books from another series! Call 1-800-873-8635 or visit www.ReaderService.com.**

---

*Terms and prices subject to change without notice. Prices do not include sales taxes, which will be charged (if applicable) based on your state or country of residence. Canadian residents will be charged applicable taxes. Offer not valid in Quebec. This offer is limited to one order per household. Books received may not be as shown. Not valid for current subscribers to the Love Inspired or Love Inspired Suspense series. All orders subject to approval. Credit or debit balances in a customer's account(s) may be offset by any other outstanding balance owed by or to the customer. Please allow 4 to 6 weeks for delivery. Offer available while quantities last.

**Your Privacy**—Your information is being collected by Harlequin Enterprises ULC, operating as Harlequin Reader Service. For a complete summary of the information we collect, how we use this information and to whom it is disclosed, please visit our privacy notice located at corporate.harlequin.com/privacy-notice. From time to time we may also exchange your personal information with reputable third parties. If you wish to opt out of this sharing of your personal information, please visit readerservice.com/consumerchoice or call 1-800-873-8635. **Notice to California Residents**—Under California law, you have specific rights to control and access your data. For more information on these rights and how to exercise them, visit corporate.harlequin.com/california-privacy.

LIRLIS22R3